# Shattered Lives

## ALLAN HUDSON

Editor: Sandra Bunting
Cover: Mark Young Designs

South Branch Scribbler
3469 Route 535, Cocagne, NB Canada E4R 3E5
www.southbranchscribbler.ca

Paperback ISBN – 978-1-988291-11-6

# ALSO BY ALLAN HUDSON

**THE DRAKE ALEXANDER SERIES:**

DARK SIDE OF A PROMISE

WALL OF WAR

**DET. JO NAYLOR SERIES:**

SHATTERED FIGURINE

**A BOX OF MEMORIES** – A COLLECTION OF SHORT STORIES

**THE ALEXANDERS 1911 -1920 VOL. 1** – HISTORICAL FICTION

## DARK SIDE OF A PROMISE

*"The best novel I've read in a long time. Highly recommended."* - SIMONNE CORMIER

## WALL OF WAR

*"A magnificent discovery leads Drake Alexander and his team to follow a trail of greed and murder in this excellent crime-solving novel. Kudos to Allan Hudson for a fast-paced, intriguing page turner."* - LISETTE LOMBARD – AUTHOR OF EBO

## SHATTERED FIGURINE

*"Fantastic read. Allan is a great wordsmith to say the least. For such a small book, it packs a heck of a wallop."* - PIERRE ARSENEAULT – AUTHOR OF POPLAR FALLS: THE DEATH OF CHARLIE BAKER

## A BOX OF MEMORIES

*"I was anxious to see where Hudson's imagination would take me next, and I wasn't disappointed even once. A Box of Memories gets my highest recommendation."* - MARK PIPER -AUTHOR OF THE OLD BLOCK

## THE ALEXANDERS 1911 -1920 VOL. 1

*"Mr. Hudson weaves a wonderful tale of love and endurance and it is easy to become entwined with Dominic and those he meets along the way. I look forward in anticipation to the next chapter in the life of the Alexanders."* - SHARON BEDDOES

# DEDICATION

This story is dedicated to the ladies that made me what I am — the good parts, at least.

Beatrice (RIP)
Frances
Shirley
Carol
June

*"Call it a clan, call it a network, call it a tribe, call it a family: whatever you call it, whoever you are, you need one."*

*Jane Howard*

# CONTENTS

# ACKNOWLEDGMENTS

As always, I'm forever indebted to my partner in life, Gloria Hudson. She continues to offer encouragement and inspiration.

To my family, Adam, Chris & Mireille, Mark & Georgette, Matthieu, Natasha, Eva, Mia, Damien and Leo – thank you for your support.

Much thanks to Allen & Gracia Williston for always being there.

A special thanks to Sandra Bunting, my editor. It's been a treat working with you.

Thanks to Mark Young Designs for the cover.

And a special thanks to you –you wonderful, fantastic readers and supporters.

# CHAPTER 1

## JANUARY 5

It was not Jo Naylor that stepped off the plane five days ago in Thailand. Here she's Jo Delany and she has no plans to ever be found again. Only two people know where she is - two people she trusts unquestioningly.

When she lands at the airport in Bangkok on New Year's Day, she stays at the Plaza Palace her first night, the one extravagance she allows herself stepping into a new segment of her life. But at $400 a night Canadian, she isn't long moving into a more modest forty-bucks-a-sleep on Dindaeng Road. Today she closes the deal for a cottage in Khiri Khan Province on the Kra Isthmus, a land bridge that connects mainland Asia with the Malay Peninsula. The village is also called Kiri Khan. An air force base nearby should make for many restaurants and bars and an interesting nightlife.

The Thai people are warm and friendly, Jo sees smiling faces everywhere. She wonders about that because sometimes she notices that although lips are smiling, the eyes are not. She knows that Thai people are big on families and their religion. You should never touch anyone's head, as it is a show of disrespect. Nor should you use your feet in any other manner other than to walk on because they are seen as dirty and low. It is uncommon to see people cry, or yell or show emotional displays in public, no outward holding hands, hugging or touching. Status is everything. She notices that people often bow or lower their heads to someone deemed to be of higher status. She hopes she doesn't make any clumsy mistakes.

Where she's staying now, there is a shopping mall a ten-minute walk away. It offers a bank and a travel agency amongst other retail outlets. Jo intends to withdraw a large amount of cash and meet a lady named Kannika at the book café across the street from the mall. Like most Thai people, she has a nickname and goes by Nika, a diminutive of her name given by her father when she was little. The money will be used for a six-month lease for the cottage, from Nika's cousin of course. Everyone has many cousins here.

Arriving early before the stores open, she glances at her image in the store windows, thinking how becoming her new dress is. Jo is lean and tanned, fit from her daily runs on the beach pounding bad thoughts into the packed sand. Leaving her shoulders bare, the dress flows to her ankles, stopping just a breath away from her flat leather sandals. The dress has a turquoise background adorned with large navy, coral and yellow palm trees that compliment the brunette locks just touching her collarbone. The soft fabric clings in the right spots without being showy. A peach shoulder bag, hand woven from hemp fibers, hangs at her waist. Stepping closer, she sees the confidence in her dark eyes. Smiling at the image, she comments aloud.

"Wouldn't the boys at the station like to see me come to work in this outfit".

The statement causes an elderly couple to hasten their steps past her, looking at her with questioning brows, worried about this *farang,* this odd westerner. Jo responds by covering her mouth and giggling but it soon turns into a frown. She is reminded of the one thing she regrets, leaving her job as a detective. She misses solving crimes with her partner Adam Thorne, her house, her friends… and her name.

She's spent the last five months in Panama recovering from the crazed attempt on her life, compounded by the aftershocks, pain and misery of her father's crimes, and ultimately her own criminal behavior. The warm breezes, the translucent waters, the scent of the brine foaming on the white sanded shores, the quiet and solitude of the moments she spent contemplating her future have all been restorative, a balm she applied daily.

Looking at the calendar this morning, she counted one hundred and fifty-seven days since her father committed suicide - with a fork - the one she paid the night attendant to leave in his padded cell at the Institute for the Criminally Insane. She's never regretted it for one second. But now she's on the run, wanted for questioning back in Canada.

When she decided upon the life changing events leading to her last days in Canada, she moved her inheritance to a bank in the Antilles, and from there to a bank in Panama. It was a legacy from her grandparents that if used wisely means she never has to work for at least ten years. By then she'll be forty-four and either forgiven or forgotten.

It takes twenty minutes and an English-Thai translation app on her phone to get the 30,000 baht in her purse. Almost twenty thousand is a half-year's rent for a seaside chalet. A thousand Canadian dollars! A good deal she tells herself. She's only seen pictures of it and the beach area but can't wait to settle in. Before going there she also needs a laptop. She decides she's going to write crime novels.

Coming out of the bank, a little girl scampers from the front window she's obviously been staring into. Stopping at the end of the mall ten storefronts away, she disappears. But she soon peeks around the wall at Jo by furtively moving one eye and a few dirty strands of hair. Jo's skin flushes with a pang of sympathy for her.

Jo remembers when she first saw her. She was going through the dumpster beside a restaurant and was shooed away by one of the staff. Jo followed her to find her huddled inside an abandoned and damaged cement pipe jumbled with others at a construction yard. Crawling through a fence in the back, Jo approached the ruins and singled out the girl's dwelling among the other populated forgotten structures. The main theme was casual cardboard. The smell was the worse, something between urine and unwashed bodies. When Jo moved the ragged curtain open, the girl shinnied to the back, eyes displaying fear. Kneeling at the entrance, Jo's smile brightened up the dim space. She talked patiently with soothing words to the girl but got no response. Jo figured she didn't understand English. Beckoning for the girl to follow, Jo's soft smile spoke of comfort. She led her back to the same restaurant, motioning for her to wait on a bench outside the door. She purchased a boxed meal and presented it to the little girl. Jo sat on one end of the bench watching the little girl wolf down the meal. She then wrapped the paper and cardboard together and placed it in a bin. Bowing, the first slight smile graced the girl's lips. Then she turned and ran.

Jo waits for her at the same place every day since but she didn't show. She doesn't want to intrude on her privacy but the little girl's wellbeing nags at Jo, enough that she ventures to the construction site in search of her. Jo thinks she can't be more than ten or eleven years old.

When she arrives, a forty-something-year-old man is trying to drag the girl from her makeshift home. He is dressed in a suit coat a size too large and stained on the shoulders, His shoes are dusty and the knees of his trouser are smudged with dirt. Thinning hair tops his sweaty head, big ears protruding. In a high-pitched voice, he is shouting something that sounds urgent and angry. He has the girl by one ankle and Jo can see that she is naked from the waist down. Jo is raging and is just about to step up to the man, when the girl kicks him in the groin with her free foot. He staggers backwards in pain, directly into Jo's path. Startled by the appearance of the foreigner, he tries to withdraw a gun from his jacket pocket but Jo is too fast for him. From the experience of all her years of training as a cop, she has him pinned to the ground in ten seconds. She kicks him again in the groin and stomps on his midsection. He groans and crawls into a fetal position. Jo finishes by kicking him in the head and into oblivion.

The little girl grabs her faded trousers and runs but not before Jo sees the bruises on the inside of the girl's thighs. She is fuming. Forgetting the girl temporarily, she removes all the man's clothing, except his underwear. She won't touch that if her life depends on it. She leaves him knowing he will suffer immense loss of face. She searches his pockets, tossing the contents and clothing in a dumpster, keeping only the wallet, the gun and an extra magazine. The only items of interest in the wallet are several business cards, a Mastercard, fifty thousand bahts and a picture of the same man, a woman and three kids in what Jo guesses vary in ages from four to nine. Tossing it into the dumpster, she pockets the business cards in her jeans pocket, leaves the credit card where someone will find it, someone dishonest she hopes, and drops the money into the cup of a beggar on the next street over. She worries about the girl and is glad she showed up today.

The child is uncertain she can trust the stranger. Yet she saved her from the terrible man. Jo waves for her to come forward and walks slowly toward her. People come and go, early shoppers chattering in their native tongue. Most avoid the girl. Some frown at her. Her jeans are mud stained on the cuffs and a few inches too short. The light brown T-shirt she wears is soiled and baggy. Her bare feet are dirty and callused. Strands of thin hair hang loosely about her head, stringy and unwashed. Smudges of something dark graces her thin cheeks. Her skin tone and face structure seem Caucasian but her oriental eyes gleam, small pools of anticipation. Considering her plight, the smile is uneasy. She stops four steps away and with hands hanging at her side, she looks up at Jo.

They stare at each other for a few moments. People move around them eyeing Jo suspiciously and regarding the waif with annoyance. Jo bends so her gaze is level with the girl.

"Do you understand English?"

The girl nods her head.

"A little."

"Don't you have a home you can go to?"

No answer. Just a shake of her head, the smile gone, eyes downcast. Jo feels sorry for the girl but is not sure if she can trust her answers. The street kids are usually begging for money or involved in some type of scam against foreigners. Yet she senses something different about this one, something that keeps her in her own little world.

"Where is your mother?"

The little girl looks up at Jo.

"My *mae* dead. Many months ago."

Jo's heart beats faster. The sadness in the small face touches her.

"And your father?"

The shoulders come up. She can't answer because she doesn't know.

"He gone. Long time."

Jo bends lower so that she's sitting on her heels and offers her best smile.

"Who was that man yesterday?"

The girl's hangs her head and blushes, her eyes pooling when she looks back up at Jo.

"When my *mae* die, people take me to his house. He keep many boys and girls but not nice. He try to hurt me before and I run away."

Jo wants to cry too; she's feeling so bad for the child. She has to help her somehow.

"You understand the word *trust?* Do you trust me?"

Another nod.

"Can I trust you?"

The head bobs enthusiastically. No one ever shows her kindness.

*"Chai, chai."*

Jo's been here long enough to know the girl is saying yes.

"Are you hungry? Would you like to come with me and we can get you cleaned up and some better clothes? And then we can find you a better place to stay."

The little girl backs off, shaking her head. A fearful shadow covers her eyes.

*"Maichai.* No better place. My place good. People there help me. Don't hurt me. They try yesterday but he wave gun at them."

Jo stands and puts both hands out, palms open.

"Okay, okay. We'll talk about that after. Come with me. I'm going to the bookstore across the street to meet a lady. It'll only take me a few minutes. Let's go back to my room but first let's get you some new clothing. What's your name?"

*"Sukhon* - but I am called *Dek Lek."*

Jo picks up the rhythm of the name and pronounces it several times.

"My name is Jo. Now come with me."

Taking the girl's hand, Jo leads her to one of the farthest stores in the mall, an anchor store that carries a variety of items, young girl's clothing one of them. If Jo is uncertain of the girl's future, at least she's going to make it a bit easier. From a noodle street vendor, Dek Lek chooses the *phat si-io* dish of veggies and noodles dark with soy sauce. Jo shakes her head at the choice because she's had it before and found it too spicy for her. Leaving the child on a bench with her fork and throwaway dish of noodles, Jo goes shopping.

Guessing at the sizes, she purchases sneakers, socks, underwear, sturdy pants, shorts, T-shirts, a water bottle, a change purse and a small Cinderella-themed backpack. Feeling hopeful, she adds a couple of pairs of pajamas. She returns to find Dek Lek sitting on the same bench, hands tucked under her legs that are swinging back and forth just short of the ground. She gestures for her to follow her and heads back to the hotel. Dek Lek is talkative now.

By the time the bath has rinsed the grit from Dek Lek, and she is clothed in new duds, Jo knows the father is British, in and out of their lives. No other family. Very poor. Mother dying from something in her lungs. Runaway from foster home last summer. A doll named Piti. Vanilla is her favorite flavor and she likes playing hide-and-seek. Del Lek means small child. She'll be ten in March. She hasn't been in school since she ran away. Jo finds her quite smart for a nine-year-old.

Jo mixes fibs and truths to Dek Lek; she's from Canada, her parents are also deceased, she likes walking and seeing new places. Root beer pop is the best. She loves books, and she worked for a small city, meeting people until she saved up enough money to go on a long holiday. Dek Lek doesn't need to know that she was a cop, that she can shoot a gun, that she can a kill a man with her bare hands. And especially that when she was looking for a serial killer, she found out it was her father.

The T-shirt is a bit too big. The extras are folded and put in the pack. As the sun starts to sink, the two sit on the couch and watch cartoons on an English television channel. Dek Lek nurses a bottle of Pepsi. Finally, when Elmer Fudd stutters "Th… th… that's all folks", Jo turns the TV off and faces Dek Lek.

"Now, what are we going to do with you? You can stay here tonight on the couch and we can decide something tomorrow."

"I stay with you."

Jo sits back on the couch to contemplate. Loneliness comes with her new life package and she doesn't always like being alone. Thinking that she could make a difference in the girl's life, and selfishly, the girl could make her life in a foreign country easier, she agrees. She takes the girl's hand and smiles.

"Okay, for now you stick with me and we'll have a little holiday and then we can decide what's best."

# CHAPTER 2

The shoreline is like a bowl, with sides stretching as far as the eye can see on either side. This section has similar cottages, most privately-owned or rentals. The northern portion offers high rises, tourist destinations, and the air force base which can be seen in the distance. The south includes retail outlets, honky-tonks, restaurants, residences and businesses in a mixture of new and old. Palm trees sway in the breeze like frenzied worshipers. Dark red meranti trees stand among lofty beeches and tropical hopea sangals that surround the many buildings. Lotus plants are common and the rose, pink or white plants have a delicate, sweet fruity scent that hitchhikes on the wind.

Jo's cottage sits thirty steps from the turquoise waters that lap at the white sands. It rests on three-foot stilts with a teak deck and steps up to it. A thatched hip roof covers the one floor, which is divided up to make two bedrooms, a bathroom, an open kitchenette, dining area and living room. The furniture is a mixture of old and new but reeks of comfort and ease. She and Dek Lek arrived earlier today just before sunset and they watched the kaleidoscope sky until darkness sent them inside. Armed with new sheets and blankets, their luggage, a takeout pizza and a few groceries, they settle in for the night with plans to buy more supplies in the morning and explore the beach in the afternoon.

Dek Lek is enamored by the tall lady she calls Jo. Still unsure of her benefactor's intentions, she nevertheless relishes the feel of the new clothes, her clean hair and skin and having someone to care about her rather than abusing her or hurting her. Jo, on the other hand, is uncertain of the young girl's future and knows that she needs to find a suitable home for her. However, she's happy to have someone to spend time with. She's just going to take each day as it comes.

Jo has always been an early riser and sits outside in the grayness of the coming day on her deck with a cup of coffee. The sun rises onto her back and she watches the morning brighten her new home on the ebbing water. Mesmerized by the tiny waves that lick the sand, she concentrates on her to-do list.

Jo is wearing a new T- shirt, with a Canadian flag on the front, a pair of khaki walking shorts and leather flip flops. Her hair is tied back in her favourite pony tail with the ends sticking out of the back of her navy baseball cap with the Toronto Maple Leafs logos emblazoned on the front. No makeup; her skin is unblemished. Despite her dark, guarded look, a closed mouth smile says "I'm good".

Dek Lek is still asleep. Her first night with Jo was uneasy, waking up a couple times disoriented, often crying from bad dreams. Jo had to lie by her side until she slept. Thankfully there were no disturbances in the night or in the girl's active mind.

As soon as Dek Lek rises they share a small breakfast with the few groceries they have. They will head north towards the shopping district and to get a haircut for Dek Lek. Going back into the cottage, Jo pours another cup of coffee and picks up her latest book – *Steal It All* – by Canadian author Chuck Bowie. She feels an infinity with the main character, a thief for hire. Someone that walks the line between right and wrong but with their heart in the proper place. She discovered the book from one of her Facebook friends from New Brunswick, back in Canada. She has since closed that account and all other connections to Jo Naylor.

After fifteen pages, she hears the toilet flush inside and soon Dek Lek appears on the deck with and questioning eyes and her dark brown hair askew. She's wearing her new cotton pajamas, the ones with the little kittens and puppies cavorting on the cloth. She walks tentatively to Jo's side.

"Good morning Dek Lek. Are you feeling ok?"

"Hi Jo. I sleep good. I hungry now."

"Me too. Let's go have some toast and peanut butter. You like peanut butter?"

She nods and smiles.

"Ok, you go wash up, comb your hair and get changed. Wear the new shorts with the little elephants on the pockets, the white T-shirt and your sneakers."

Dek Lek skips back through the open door and into her bedroom. Jo adds bread to the toaster and fetches the butter and peanut butter to make breakfast. While digging out a knife from the utensil drawer, she's disturbed by a scream from the bathroom. Dropping everything on the cupboard, she rushes to the bathroom to find Dek Lek standing on the toilet bowel with her hands over her mouth and intently gazing at something moving on the floor by the corner of the linen closet.

A small snake with an olive tail and dark-brown-edged scales, as scared as the young girl, squirms its way back into the closet. Unknown to Jo, it's a juvenile Indo-Chinese rat snake, totally harmless. She doesn't care for snakes and is uncertain if this one is venomous. She opens the closet door gently to see where it went and spots the tail disappearing into a small hole chewed in the corner of the closet that opens to the ground underneath. Reaching for a face cloth, she plugs the hole. Turning back to Dek Lek, she hugs the girl.

"There, now he… or she, can't get back in. Don't worry."

"I don't like… *ngu*… they scare me."

"It's called a snake in English and it was just a little one. Before we go, we'll check around and make sure there aren't any more. You okay now?"

Another nod.

"Well then finish up and come eat."

After breakfast, Jo and Dek Lek clean up the plates and utensils with Jo showing Dek Lek how to wash them properly and explaining how she likes to keep things neat and clean. They head out for the store a little after nine and talk about how Dek Lek would like to have her hair cut. The sidewalk is in shade most of the time with tall palms trees lining the road. The sun has crested the trees and promises a cloud free day. The street is active for a Saturday. Pedestrians on both sides scurry with shopping bags or small children in tow. Jo loves the straight bangs on the little boys, the roughed-up knees of the little girls wearing dresses. A fifteen-minute walk brings them to a Tesco Lotus grocery store. Signs in both Thai and English welcome them, offering both western and Thai foodstuffs. A cart is soon half filled with necessities and a few extras. Jo has allowed Dek Lek to pick the desserts and is surprised by her choice of ginger snaps, never one of her favourites. A few mangoes and Durian sticky rice also make it into the basket.

After making arrangements for the groceries to be delivered, the girls go to a hairdressing shop whose sign shows both a boy and a girl and a pair of scissors. They enter to find a busy establishment full of waiting men, ladies and children. There are four other patrons before them. To pass the time they leaf through some style magazines from a crowded rack on the wall. Dek Lek points to a photo of a young girl with curls to her chin with the top swept over, held by a small butterfly clip. Her hair has a natural wave and they decide this will look nice. Dek Lek clutches the magazine and shows it to the stylist when she sits up in the chair. Jo decides to get hers cut too. Before she can change her mind, she chooses a short style over the ears with a tapered back. The top is left spikey and care-free. The hat goes into the back pocket.

Walking back, each with a cone dripping with melting ice cream, they laugh at some of Dek Lek's antics while trying to survive on her own, the time she found a twenty thousand Bhatt on the beach, the time she chased an old man away from her hut, crazy things! When they are less than a quarter mile from the cottage, a woman bursts through the foliage on the beach side of the road. She is sobbing and wailing and bleeding from a cut lip. Her blouse is torn in the front exposing a white bra. Her capris are damp up to the waist, her knees smudged with wet sand. She shrieks loudly in what sounds to Jo as Thai gibberish and falls at their feet. With tears streaking her face, she crawls to clutch Jo's ankles. Two ladies behind them hasten away. A young couple turn aside. There is no one else nearby.

*"Pord chwy chan dwy…* "(Please help me, please…)

Jo doesn't understand what she is saying. Bending to comfort the woman, she asks Dek Lek to translate. The woman sits back on her heels, wiping her eyes with the sleeve of her shirt. The two speak urgently. Jo offers the woman a cotton handkerchief she normally carries. Dek Lek is overcome by the woman's tale. When she turns to tell Jo, her eyes are glazed with shining pools.

"Someone take her daughter, her little girl. Two men, bad men. She want you to help."

Jo steps back, hands on her chest.

"Me? I don't know how I can help her. Tell her we'll find the police."

Dek Lek translates and the woman shakes her head violently. She looks at Jo with pleading eyes but speaks to Dek Lek, knowing the lady doesn't understand her language.

"She say no police. Many police bad, do same thing, steal little girls and boys. Sell them. She say maybe you help."

"That's terrible. I don't know how I can help. But let's get her up. Where's her husband?"

"Husband?"

"Yes, her man."

Dek Lek explains to the woman who tells her husband works on a ship.

"He work on big boat, gone many weeks."

"Okay, we'll take her with us, get her settled down and find out what happened."

Jo helps her up while Dek Lek talks reassuringly. They proceed to the cottage. Jo offers support and listens as the woman, shaking and crying, tries to explain the situation to Dek Lek. Passersby are avoiding the public outburst, which they find embarrassing.

By the time they get to the cottage they have a good idea of what has happened. Jo gets her in the bathroom, cleans up her split lip and offers her a T- shirt to wear. It's an older, plain white one. She knows she won't get it back but that's ok. The woman is sitting on the couch with a half empty bottle of water staring in a stupor at the floor. Dek Lek does the best she can to relay what she heard to Jo.

The woman, whose name is Preeda and her daughter whose name is Malai, come from a small village inland and arrived this morning by bus only an hour ago. Her daughter wanted to walk on the beach before they went to the stores. Her mother was sitting on the sand watching her wade in the water when two men approached on a fast boat. They were trying to wrestle the girl into the boat when the mother attacked the man in the water who was struggling with her daughter. Another man hit her and tore her blouse. She lost her balance and fell in the water and the two men got away.

Jo drills the woman for clues. Once a cop, always a cop some people say and that's true with Jo.

"Ask her which way they went."

Dek Lek points north.

"She say they go that way, toward where planes are."

Jo is confused as the airport is not in that direction. Dek Lek corrects her.

"No, where army has planes."

"Oh yes, the air force, not the army."

"Ask her to describe the men."

While Dek Lek gets the description, Jo grabs her note pad off the table where she wrote her grocery list earlier and hastily jots down the details. One man was very skinny, not too tall with long hair and a crooked nose, wearing a green T-shirt and baggy pants. The other man is the one that assaulted her - taller, bigger with a scruffy beard, a patch on one eye and many tattoos on his hands and arms, He was wearing a light brown shirt with pockets and funny things on the shoulders. He now has several scratch marks on his face from the mother's long nails.

"She say she try to pull man back by grabbing his shirt but that when he hit her."

Jo thinks the funny things on the shoulders can possibly be epaulets but as she doesn't know how to translate that word, she keeps it to herself. Jo's knows the bigger man would stand out in a crowd but and there's always a large crowd in Kiri Khan.

"Ask her what the boat looked like."

The woman shrugs her shoulders and shakes her head.

"She not sure Jo, wasn't looking for it. She knows it have white and black marks on the side. When it take off, she see large letters on back but mostly covered by big motor. She see FA, that all."

"Ask her if the black marks looked like painted lines."

Shaking head and hands waving, the woman explains that the lines were not straight.

"Not paint, more like…, I can't think of right word…"

Jo thinks of a white boat rubbing up against rubber tires that are sometimes used as bumpers on some wharfs.

"Like streaks Dek Lek? Like big scratch marks?""

Dek Lek confers again.

"Yes, like scratch marks."

"Can she guess how big it was?"

The woman is thinking, not sure how to answer. She points to one wall which is a little more than five feet away and then to the other side of the room, another five or six feet.

"She say as long as this room, maybe a little more."

Jo sits down on an easy chair to the left of the woman and Dek Lek on the couch and peers out the window at the water. Both the woman and Dek Lek can see she's deep in thought and leave her undisturbed. Jo speaks up after a few minutes of thought.

"Did she have a purse or bags?"

"No, no purse or bag, she scared someone steal. Carry money in pocket."

"Does she have a place to stay tonight?"

"She want to know why you ask that?"

The cop in Jo kicks in and she loves nothing more than looking for clues. She knows she's totally out of her element here but has an idea of where to start.

"Tell her you and I are going to look for her daughter."

# CHAPTER 3

By noon Jo and Dek Lek have taken Preeda to a cousin's house. He's a head shorter than Jo, a shy man with small ears and a thin moustache. Middle aged like Preeda, she finds they look about the same age. The wife is round and all smiles. Five or six kids are playing in the yard with it being a Saturday and no school. The house is inland from the beach and looks much too small for all the people in might contain. However, they welcome Preeda and fuss over her about her daughter missing. Jo has a cellular phone as does the man so they exchange numbers. Jo stores his number in the contacts portion of her phone under his name, Kiet. Preeda gives her a photo of her daughter, taken at school two years ago. She tells Dek Lek that her hair is longer now and she has a scar on her chin where she fell on a chair last summer.

Jo is wearing black cotton trousers, sturdy hiking boots, a white T-shirt and a plain black baseball hat with a frayed peak, one of her favorites with no logo. Across one shoulder is a tan, slim leather strap holding a small purse on the opposite side. She decided she's not doing the makeup thing anymore. With Jo's smooth skin and exquisite features, she doesn't really need any. Dek Lek is similarly attired, only her trousers and T-shirt are dark blue, almost navy. Usually barefoot, she complains her new boots hurt her feet so Jo stops in the middle of the sidewalk to loosen up the laces.

"Don't tie them so tight Dek Lek, leave them loose until they are worn a bit."

Scooters and other bikes zoom along the street, leaving an odorous trail. Many need new mufflers. People scurry about, everyone in a hurry. Shops are busy.

"Where we go, Jo?"

"Well, before we left the cottage, I looked up a number and called to make an appointment to meet another lady that might be able to help us."

"Who?"

"Her name's Achara Jones. She's a private investigator."

"I don't know those words… priate what?"

"An investigator, someone who helps you find people, helps you look for them when you don't know where they are."

"Like police?"

"A little bit like police but not the same. They work by themselves most times and they don't always follow the rules."

This causes a smirk on the little girl's face.

"I think she be like you, Jo?"

Jo's laughing when she approaches a garage with mopeds for rent. Another place she found on her phone. It is a squat L-shaped building, wedged in beside a hardware store and an apartment building. Several palm trees with heavy, drooping leaves guard the back. A fenced-in area has a variety of bikes, scooters, mopeds and motorcycles and a few bicycles. Many are new, many are not. A rough table sits inside the open wire gate, which was even with the sidewalk. A large umbrella is attached to its side, offering shaded respite from the afternoon sun. Stepping under it they confront an angular man, all arms and neck. His head looks like it might fall over. He smiles at them, showing two missing front teeth. His upper lip flaps when he speaks. making it take a huge effort not to laugh.

Jo points to a shiny yellow scooter in the fenced in area behind the man and instructs Dek Lek to tell him she wants to rent it, to pay to use it for the rest of the day and maybe tomorrow too. After Dek Lek makes inquiries, the man's head is shaking. He turns in his seat, a backless piano stool and points at a red one. Dek Lek translates.

"He say yellow not for rent, for sale. Best deal is red one, work good. Better for you with long legs."

Jo moves around the table and over to the scooter. The paint has a few chips but it's quite clean, no stains on the long black seat, big enough for both of them. Jo eyes the simple controls, brakes on the left of the handlebar, accelerator on the right. An automatic. She likes it. She looks at Dek Lek.

"Ask him, how much for two days, two helmets and insurance too?"

Dek Lek doesn't understand helmets until Jo mimes with her hands. She relays Jo's request. The man goes on for a moment until Del Lek starts arguing with him. Both of them have their hands waving, their voices shrill. It goes on for a couple of minutes until the man breaks into a toothless grin and offers his hand to Dek Lek to seal the deal. She turns to Jo.

"He want 1000 baht. But I tell him if he want to rob people, he not a nice man. Nice man would only charge 400 baht for two days and everything else. He decide to be nice man."

Jo tries to conceal her giggles as she passes the money.

After leaving her passport number, her address, signing the rental agreement and showing the man that she knows how to operate the scooter,

Jo and Dek Lek move into the flow of the traffic and head north toward the Air Force base. While she is being cautious, other scooters zoom past her, waving their hands and glaring in displeasure. The office for the PI is three kilometers away, beyond, but not far from, the military base. The temperature is slightly higher than normal at twenty-eight degrees Celsius, the sun shining in a cloudless sky. The light breeze from the scooter provides some relief from the heat.

Achara Jones has an office on the second floor of a building on Thanonsuesuk Road, next to a Muslim restaurant. She is expecting Jo at 1:30 p.m. Jo pulls the scooter into a vacant spot near the restaurant and decides to leave the scooter there as she sees other bikes parked there. Carrying their helmets, the two enter the building. They see a sign in Thai and English which directs them to the second level and office number 201A. The door to the office has opaque glass window with a small plastic plate under it announcing that they've arrived at 201A. After tapping gently on the door, they hear a confident voice call out "*Khaomasi*". (Come in)

Stepping into the office, Jo is surprised by the décor, all pink and lady like. She was expecting something darker and foreboding given the profession of the occupant. But then again, she's never been in a PI's office before. The small narrow room contains a cluttered desk, two beige filing cabinets on the left, an open door to an inner office on the right. A sofa with soft cushions is by the wall on the left. A small table in front holds a few magazines, a coloring book and crayons and a vase with plastic flowers. Several prints of seascapes in silver frames hang on the walls. Behind the desk, the wall is mostly taken up with a cork bulletin board with not much cork showing. On it are post-it-notes, wanted posters, lists, photos of menacing looking people and whatnot. The same voice calls out again from the inner office.

"Is that you Ms. Delaney?"

"Yes, it is."

"Have a seat and I'll be with you in a minute. I'm on the phone."

"Ok."

Jo and Dek Lek take a seat on the sofa. Dek Lek opens the coloring book to a new page and starts filling in the lines on an anime character. Jo holds her hands in her lap and looks around. What catches her eye is the photo of a handgun. From the extra cross pin above the trigger, the finger grooves and accessory rail, Jo recognizes it as a Glock 17, third generation. It's a 1980 model, a good gun Jo thinks. Uses standard NATO 9x19 parabellum ammo with 17 bullets in the magazine. Her former captain carried one.

When Jo spoke to her on the phone earlier, she envisioned a tiny woman from the soft voice but was she wrong. Achara Jones stands just under six feet, a lean and solid build, tight curly hair and flattish nose of a black parent. Thai features are also eminent, wider cheek bones, flawless skin the color of wet sand and the fold of the eyes, the dark pools which give away nothing. A slender scar runs across her left temple, it's tail just under the hairline. Even though her mien suggests you shouldn't mess with her, all in all, Achara Jones is a beautiful woman. Jo guesses her to be close to her age.

Achara's wearing dark slacks and polo shirt under a light linen jacket. Extending her hand, she greets Jo who stands. It's then that Jo notices the pistol under the left arm with the handle sticking out of a soft holster. She sees that it's a Glock – like the picture.

"Hi there. I'm Achara. Can I call you Jo?"

The handshake is firm and short.

"Yes, please do."

Pointing at Dek Lek who is engrossed in coloring and being a normal little girl, she raises her brows in question. Jo smiles and looks down at the young girl.

"This is Dek Lek, say hello to Achara, honey."

Dek Lek looks up and offers a wee smile and nods but goes back to the image that is getting greener by the minute.

"Your daughter?"

Jo shakes her head.

"No, just someone I'm looking after for a while."

Achara goes behind the desk where a small refrigerator is situated and removes a bottle of water. Twisting the cap loose, she sets it beside Dek Lek and smiles down at her.

Dek Lek blushes at the woman's kindness.

"*Khopkhun.*" (Thank you)

"You're welcome, little one."

"Would you like one Jo?"

Jo waves it off.

"No thanks."

"Well, why don't you come into my office and tell me how I can help. I normally have a secretary but she's out sick today so there's just us."

She leads Jo into the other office while Dek Lek continues to color. Jo is surprised by the starkness of the office - beige walls, a large window on the outer wall with blinds at half-mast protecting the room from the sun. There are no prints, no ornaments, only a grey metal desk with a chair and two leather seats in front and an air conditioner humming white noise in the corner window. A credenza stands behind the desk against the wall, piled high with folders and writing pads on one side and a desktop computer on the other, everything in order. The only items on the desk are another writing pad, several pencils, an old-fashioned dial phone, a clock and the back of a picture frame with the photo facing Achara. Jo points at the phone.

"I haven't seen one of those for some time."

Achara pulls a cell phone from her back pocket and waves it at Jo.

"It's a decoration only. It works but I rarely use it. It belonged to my grandmother and I hang on to it for memory's sake. Now, what can I do for you? But before you start, I don't do spousal spying."

Jo laughs and shrugs it off. Removing the photo from the small purse she carries she passes it to Achara.

"No spouse so no worries on that part. The reason I'm here is…"

Jo explains what happened earlier that day, the woman pleading for help, how her daughter was abducted, what she did and why she came.

Achara sits back in her chair, studies the photo for a minute and eyes Jo suspiciously. Looks her up and down, studies her face.

"Why are you pursuing this? What's in this for you?"

"Nothing is in it for me other than helping this woman get her daughter back."

"And you think you can?"

"I'm familiar with finding people, so why not?"

"You are? How so?"

Jo hesitates, not sure how much to give away of her past.

"Well, with an in heritance, I decide to travel and see the world. I was a police officer for twelve years and the youngest detective in our team. And to be truthful, I miss the chase. Thought maybe I could help this woman."

Achara thinks this over. Looks directly in Jo's eyes looking for any deception. In her trade, reading faces and mannerisms can tell her a lot. She sees no guile, no frivolity in Jo.

"Seems odd if you miss the action why you would want to give it up and travel when you're so young. Leaving something shady in the past? Wherever you're from. By the accent, Canada I assume."

"Yes, I'm Canadian."

That's the only answer she gives. Achara waits for something further but after a minute of silence, she realizes she doesn't want to dig anymore. She likes what she sees in Jo.

"All right then. What do want of me?"

"Have you ever been involved in missing children cases before?"

Achara holds up a finger, swivels her chair to face the credenza and pulls out the top drawer. Removing a handful of photos, she places them on the desk in two piles. Pointing to the smallest pile on the left that only has three photos, she looks at Jo with an angry glare.

"Those are the ones I did find; the other pile is the ones I didn't or can't and it pisses me off."

Jo picks up the thicker pile. There are seven photos of children, mainly girls, averaging in age from ten to fifteen. Jo feels a deep-rooted anger similar to what Achara is feeling. She hates it. She looks back at Achara.

"You think it has anything to do with human trafficking?"

"Is the Queen of England British? Yeah, I do. I hate the bastards that do this. I found those three because I was called in almost immediately when they were kidnapped. Strictly amateurs. I mean, there's big money in child slavery and an unhappy, miserable existence for them. The others involved in the collection you're holding were probably more professional. They're over a year old. I've given up on them. No leads, no clues, it's as if they disappeared into thin air. It kills me"

"The three you found, what was the modus operandi?"

"There were no discernable patterns, random kidnappings. One at a mall across the city, the other from the parents' front yard and the third while walking home from school, all in different locations unassociated with each other. The only thing all three had in common was that they were girls, each one was eleven years old, but I believe that was coincidental."

Jo is nodding, her mind in motion.

"Did you apprehend the perps?"

"Nope, not usually my style. There were clues and witnesses all over the place. As I said, amateurs. I found the kids and passed what I learned to a cop that I trust. Only one perp made it out alive and she's doing time in the Chiang Rai Prison."

Jo slides the photo she brought off the desk and holds it up.

"Let's get back to this girl. Here's what I know."

Jo takes a small notepad from her shoulder bag and relates what she's written to Achara who is scribbling her own notes. She looks up from her notes with raised brows when Jo finishes.

"… and it happened only this morning, less than four hours ago. Her trail should still be hot. She has to be close to here, being held somewhere."

Achara sits back again when Jo is finished.

"This is not the first time I've heard about abduction on the water. It's clever because they have a ton of places to hide out. So, where do I fit in?"

'I need someone familiar with the turf around here. I'm a stranger of course and I doubt I'd get much cooperation from the locals so I'd like to hire you and we can look together."

"I don't know about that. I work alone. Things get tight, I can't keep an eye out for someone else."

Jo sits straight, almost a twinkle in her eyes, her chin out.

"I've been in a few "tight" spots before, Achara, and I'm still here. You don't have to look out for me."

There are a few moments of silence between the women.

"I charge 3000 bahts a day, which includes most expenses. Any peripherals other than the norm you must come good for. You okay with that?"

Jo reaches into her bag and withdraws 6000 bahts, passing it to the private investigator.

"There's enough for two days. I know well enough that if we don't find her by then, we probably won't. Can you clear your workload right away?"

Achara slides the currency into a top drawer of her desk.

"You got it. What do you want to do first?"

Jo rises and shakes Achara's hand.

"Let's go look for a man with a boat who wears an eye patch."

# CHAPTER 4

Achara drives a Mitsubishi 4 x 4, dark blue with a small dent on the rear hatch. Dek Lek is in the back seat with Jo in the front passenger seat. It's parked at the rear of the building and enters the street under an overhang that joins two buildings. She looks over at Jo who is gripping the handhold over her head, not familiar with driving on the left side of the road like in England. Achara pulls into the street, weaving into traffic like a dog that doesn't know its place in the pack.

"Where to?"

Jo's foot is pumping the imaginary brake pedal at her feet as Achara has the nose of the car near enough to the bus in front of her to read the fine print on the dealer's sticker.

"Umm, let's go back to the scene of the abduction. See if there are any clues to be found. I haven't taken the time to comb the beach yet."

"I was going to suggest that. What's the address again?"

Ten minutes later, they pull over to where the woman rushed from the shrubs. The three of them part the bushes and walk down to the beach. The tide is out and the skid mark from the boat touching shore is visible, with footprints indicating a struggle. They search the area around for a good twenty feet on either side, carefully watching where they step in the event something has fallen. After fifteen minutes, they're about to give up when Dek Lek bends to the sand where something shiny catches her eye. Scooping it from the sand and passing it to Jo, she sees it's a metal button the size of a Canadian nickel. Achara takes it and studies it closer.

"Hmm, that's odd."

"What is it Achara?"

Pointing out the embossment on the button, they see an anchor with scroll around it and a temple above.

"It's an emblem of the Thai Navy. Perhaps it's something to go by, maybe a sailor or an ex-sailor?"

Jo remembers the conversation she had when the woman was describing the man.

"That would explain epaulets that Preeda saw on the shoulders of the shirt. She said it was dirty. I think ex-sailor. It could be something… or nothing. Maybe he found the shirt. You have any contacts in the Navy?"

Achara nods in assent and passes the button to Jo.

"Not directly but I'm in tight with someone that can. Possibly ex-Navy and an eye patch, could be something. I'll get in touch with my contact later because now he'll still be at work and he doesn't want to be disturbed there."

Jo walks to the edge of the water and gazes north.

"In a boat, where could they possibly go from here and hide a young girl?"

Achara stands beside her. Dek Lek is sitting above them on the beach drawing a starfish in the sand with her finger.

"That's a good question Jo. It'd have to be where they would have a car parked, or a building close by, or a wharf or landing spot."

"And not many people around to arouse suspicion."

"Unless the people around are in on the scheme."

"Yeah, there's that too.

"From the description of the boat you gave me, it's not a long-distance craft so I would be inclined to think it is within a mile or two from here and you say they headed north toward the Air Force base?"

They look at each other after that remark. Jo with raised eyebrows, Achara with a smirk.

"The Air Force base? Would there be somewhere near there to dock a boat and hide a girl, Achara?"

"Oh, definitely but I don't know how civilians would be able to?"

"Maybe the culprits are not all civilians. Maybe there's more to this than two men on the water?"

"Definitely, but the base would be a stretch Jo, nothing in any of my investigations pointed in that direction. I wouldn't dismiss it but I wouldn't concentrate on it."

Dek Lek has been listening to the conversation quietly, following Jo around. She tugs on Jo's sleeve and points to another boat that is gliding off shore.

"Maybe we get a boat and look."

Achara pats Dek lek on the shoulder.

"There's an idea. Maybe we have a young detective in the making. Right Jo?"

"That's a great idea, Dek Lek."

The young girl blushes from the compliment. Jo raises her hands in question.

"Where could we rent one Achara?"

Achara is already heading back to her car when she waves for the other two to follow.

"We don't need to. I know where we can get one."

Jo runs to catch up.

"And you can operate it?"

"For sure. If it's got an accelerator and a way to steer it, I can drive it. If I don't know how, I'll soon learn. Let's go. It's not far from here."

# CHAPTER 5

Dek Lek is thrilled. She's never been on a boat before and certainly not one as luxurious as the craft Achara pilots away from a berth at the boat club less than a kilometer south of Jo's cottage. It's a pontoon boat with blue and white leather seats, a built-in refrigerator/cooler, the pilot's seat forward amidships, an overhead awning to keep the sun off them and two powerful engines aft. It belongs to a former lover of Achara's. She's a hundred meters offshore and heading towards the area where they were twenty minutes ago looking for clues. After discussing it, they decided to return to the abduction site and follow the shore north. Jo stands on the port bow next to the pilot's seat, watching the shoreline.

Earlier, Jo and Dek Lek followed Achara from the car in the parking lot, into the main lobby of the boat club where Achara chatted with an elderly gentleman that she obviously knows well. She speaks Thai like a native, which Jo knows from talking to her that she is not. On the way over Jo queried her on her roots. Achara's mother is Thai, her father African American. She grew up in Florida until her father passed away when she was eighteen. She and her mother moved to Thailand so they could be with her mother's family. That was seventeen years ago, making Achara one year older than Jo. Her mother lives in Bangkok with a new husband, and Achara hates him.

Obtaining the keys to the boat and a warning from the man that the boat only has a half tank of fuel and that it might be wise to top it up if they're going far. After gassing up, they moved cautiously out of the dock. Jo scans the beaches for a white boat with black smudges on the side and chats idly with Achara as they approach the area where the girl was abducted.

"This former boyfriend doesn't mind you using his boat?"

"Actually, it belongs to a former girlfriend."

She watches Jo for her reaction to this revelation. There's none.

Coming in close to shore where a private marina has a variety of watercraft tied up in different berths, Achara cuts the forward motion and lets the boat drift. Digging a pair of binoculars from a cabinet below the helm, she passes them to Jo.

"Have a look for a white skiff with black smudges."

Dek Lek is kneeling on the sofa-like seat facing the water, hand above her eyes to shade out the sun. She doesn't know what a skiff is but knows to look at any white boats. As there seems to be quite a few, she counts them thinking it might be important. Achara idles the boat closer to inspect the ones farther in. After ten minutes Jo realizes there's nothing here of interest. She scans the beach area toward the Air Force base. There is a wharf with two riverine patrol boats tied up and a naval offshore patrol vessel anchored close by. Less than three hundred meters beyond the base, there are a series of warehouses with short jetties protruding into the water. Small and medium sized boats are moored at each of the three that are visible from where they are. Jo points to them.

"Let's take a look at the warehouse piers, Achara."

Achara confirms the instructions with a nod and powers up. She loops out around the official boundary marked with buoys. Closing to a hundred meters to cruise past the warehouses. After bypassing the base, she cuts the throttle so the craft idles forward and then she moves closer to shore but not close enough to draw attention to themselves. Thankfully there are other boats - fishing boats, pleasure craft - that move along the watery highway.

The third warehouse, tall as a two-storey house and three times as long, has a roof and walls of grey corrugated metal, no signage. One corner, top right, has a loose piece of siding which waves in the breeze, drawing Jo's gaze through binoculars. Scanning the grounds, she sees two men with a forklift moving large crates piled on the wharf through an open garage size door. There are no boats moored. A car comes from between the buildings onto the wharf. Keeping her eyes glued to the vehicle, she instructs her pilot to slow down.

"Keep the boat slow Achara. Look at the gray plain building where a car just pulled in the back."

Achara puts the boat in neutral and lets it float.

"I see it now. Too far for me to see any detail. What about it?"

"I've seen it before."

Jo briefly relates the incident when she found the man tormenting and abusing Dek Lek, a car like that had been parked near the construction yard.

"I mean how many blue and white 1964 Mercedes can be there in Kiri Khan?"

Achara is thinking more of the man's tasteless actions and his reaction to Jo's aggressiveness. She stands beside Jo as the boat gently rocks, putting her hand on her shoulder to make her face her. Jo drops the binoculars.

"The bastard! But listen, you are in very deep shit, my friend. Whoever he is, he has suffered tremendous loss of face, so you'll be number one on his wanted list. Watch your back. Now, how do you know specifically it's a 1964 Mercedes?"

"My uncle had one, only it was burgundy and white. I always remember the big shiny grill and what I always thought of as a peace sign, the Mercedes hood ornament."

While the women were talking, with razor sharp youthful eyesight, Dek Lek is watching the car that Jo saw. It has been parked motionless for several minutes, before two men get out. Dek Lek is jumping up and down on the seat, pointing a shaking hand and yells out.

"Look Jo. Look at man that drive."

Picking up the binoculars Jo concentrates on the man but only sees his back as he walks toward a door at the rear of the building that is covered by a small roof. Several meters away, he stops and turns back to wave for his companion to follow and when Jo sees his face, she gasps.

"It's him, the low life after Dek Lek. That fu…"

She catches herself when Dek Lek looks up at her. The big eyes make her feel guilty. She doesn't need to hear trash from Jo.

"… that furball slime. What can he be doing here?"

Achara takes the binoculars and catches a glimpse of the man before he enters the shadow under the doorway. Like Jo, she concentrates on the driver and when the second man follows the first one through the door, Achara only sees his back and in the darkness of the overhang doesn't notice the epaulets on his shoulders.

"I know that scum. Jaru Bunnag, people call him Ru. When I was sniffing around his house for wayward children, I came up against a stone wall. Everything legit. He places kids in homes, keeps records, an adoption center more or less. I've heard rumours of him abusing the kids. He's had a few runaways. That's what he says, of course. If he's into something deeper, it's a good cover. I'd give anything to take him down."

Jo shucks her thumb toward Dek Lek.

"She's one of the runaways?"

Achara eyes the little girl with new interest. Someone who's been in the house.

"Okay. We'll save that for later. We don't know if Bunnag is involved with that girl taken today. If we don't find anything else, I think we should come back here tonight."

Jo's deductive reasoning is like a trap, and when the image of him pulling at Dek Lek's bare legs sets it off, her sixth sense snaps in.

"Good plan. Let's remember the location, and now, let's find that boat."

# CHAPTER 6

It takes them over two hours to find the boat. They cruised north for an hour, checking every jetty, makeshift pier or wharf right up to where the industrial area turned into beach. Backed by a busy street, it contained mostly businesses and homes. Giving up their search, they return to where Achara parked her car and past the ramps where people launch their watercraft. Several are being taken out or launched at the same time on the wide concrete ramp. In the center, an older dark blue Toyota truck is pulling a trailer from the water. On the trailer is a white skiff. It's Achara that points out the black streaks across the body.

"Look at black marks on that one."

Jo checks it out with the binoculars and can see where something dark has rubbed against the sides. It resembles the one Preeda described. She watches the truck pull clear of the ramp and park on the side of the street. A tall man with long stringy hair and a white sleeveless shirt gets out and crosses the street to a pizzeria. Checking her watch, Jo sees it's a little after 5:00 PM. Assuming he's going for his supper or take out, she motions for Achara to head toward shore.

"Get in close, I want to take a look."

Achara skillfully lets the big pontoons gently bump against the concrete for Jo to jump out. She runs up the ramp, and slithering down by cars and trucks parked near the ramp, she sidles over to the edge of the boat and peers over the gunwale. At the back of the boat, under the engine tipped into the boat for haulage, a young girl's bikini bottom swirls in an oily puddle of water. It's red with yellow stripes like the one Preeda's little girl was wearing. Fury runs up her back like a bolt of electricity. Her eyes go blurry with anger. Shaking her head to clear it, she creeps back between other vehicles until she can stand up, and run down the ramp where Achara is keeping the boat close. She tells Achara what she saw.

"We can't follow him if he gets back in the truck Achara. By the time you get back to your car, he could be gone. We need to question him now."

"Agreed. We need to get him in the boat where we can use a little persuasion on him. We'll have to assume he doesn't speak English so leave it to me. You watch the boat. Look here. These are all the controls you need. But before I go, here, hang on to this."

Achara reaches down to an ankle holster and withdraws a Springfield XD-S, a subcompact 9mm with eight in the mag and one in the barrel. She shows Jo the safety, where the throttle is, where the gear box is and describes how to keep the boat tight against the concrete. Leaving Jo at the helm and Dek Lek watching for anything odd, Achara jumps from the craft and saunters up the ramp to where the truck is. The vehicle is parked next to the entrance to the jetty. On the same side of the street, a short distance from the truck is a small engine repair shop. Lawnmowers and ride-on tractors are parked in the dirt driveway and a man is tinkering with a chainsaw on a bench in front. Few people are on the sidewalks. She waits at the passenger door of the truck.

She only waits another five minutes before the man with the stringy hair leaves the pizzeria with a bottle of soda in one hand and a flat cardboard box with steam escaping from the edges in the other hand. Perfect for her plan. When he nears the truck, he sets the soda on the roof while digging his keys from a front pocket. It's then that Achara catches his attention and moves to his side with a submissive smile. The man can't help notice the attractive woman and smiles back at her, a missing tooth creating a black gap in his teeth, the rest yellowed from cigarettes and coffee. She waves to him and points to the front wheel, speaking to him in Thai.

"Looks like you have a flat tire."

A frown creases his brow. Leaving the soda on the roof, he walks to the other side with the box still in his hand. When he bends to look at the tire, she steps closer and pokes her pistol into his ribs. Speaking in Thai, the smirk never leaves her face. To anyone watching, they're having a friendly conversation.

"Don't make any sudden moves or I'll put a hole in your back that I can fit that box into."

Staying stiff, the man reacts with gritted teeth.

"I don't know what you're up to lady, but this is not a good way to meet people."

"Regardless, pass me the pizza and slowly turn around."

He doesn't move.

"You won't shoot me here. Too many witnesses."

She pushes the barrel of the gun deeper and he grunts from the move.

"I already don't like you, and I know this boat has been used for illegal activities. So, do you want to gamble? Try rolling the dice to see if I won't?"

He sees the hardness in her eyes, like someone used to getting her way, a meanness that is solid. He passes her the pizza, which she takes in her free hand.

"Turn slowly towards the jetty and stay close. Walk toward the pontoon boat at the bottom."

He does as he's told. He climbs slowly into the boat, and following Jo's instructions, he sits on the edge of the seat opposite Dek Lek who is staring wide-eyed at the action. Achara places the pizza box on the floor and sits beside him with her pistol jammed into his ribcage, reminding him to stay quiet. Jo reverses the craft slowly away from the jetty, moving hundreds of meters off shore. When they are out of the traffic lane, Jo cuts the throttle to idle, puts it in neutral and lets the boat float. She motions for Achara and the man to slide over and jams her own gun into the ribcage on the man's opposite side. He visibly gulps and starts to sweat. He knows he's in trouble. Achara backs off a bit and starts questioning him.

"There was a little girl abducted by men in your boat this morning. Where is she?"

"It's not my boat. I don't know anything about a little girl."

Achara sees the lie in his eyes. Using her gun, she slashes the man in the face, leaving a deep red mark and a long scratch on his cheek. His head thrashes against the leatherette of the seat and his hand goes to his face. His auto reaction to strike out is tempered by Jo's gun poking into his side.

"We're not fucking around here. We're running out of time. I'm going to ask you again. Where's the little girl?"

The man is a coward interested now only in saving his own skin. His hands shake. Dek Lek stares open-mouthed at the trio.

"I... I don't know where she is. I only take care of the boat, move it around."

"Where do they keep the kids?"

"I swear lady I don't know."

Achara raises her gun to strike again and the man cowers against the seat visibly afraid. Achara questions him more about the kids, their abduction. He's either very good at playing dumb or he really doesn't know anything. She backs off.

"Who you working for?"

"Bunnag."

"Who else?'

"I don't know the others. He meets with someone from the base sometimes but I'm never included. I'm nobody in this circus. I fix engines, repair cars, boats, bikes whatever."

"Where you taking the boat?"

He points down towards the warehouses, directly at the one they saw Bunnag at earlier. Achara explains the conversation to Jo.

"Ask him if he can get us in there, Achara."

She does and the man rants while shaking his head. Achara translates.

"He says there are too many people there. It is a working warehouse and he has limited access to the workshop in the front. He doesn't know what takes place in the back."

"Think he's telling the truth?"

"I can't be sure but I've been reading people for a long time and I think it's safe to say he doesn't know anything about the kids. He's a maintenance man. I don't think he's a player."

She moves closer and levels the gun between his eyes. He trembles.

"How can we get in there at night?"

"Good luck with that. The back section is locked up tighter than a rat's ass. The only access to the front workshop is through the sliding door, which is bolted from the inside. Entry might be possible through a side entrance that has shaky lock but that would only get you in the garage section."

"Any alarms?"

"None that I know of. I don't know about the back."

Leaving the man sitting there nursing his sore face, Achara waves Jo and Dek Lek to the front of the boat out of earshot. Jo keeps her eyes and weapon trained on the man and he knows it. Although he was patted down, he carries a knife in his left boot that Achara missed. Bending forward holding his head in his hand trying to stem the trickle of blood from the scratch on his cheek, his left hand goes slowly to his boot, unseen by Jo who is on his right side. It's Dek Lek that states the obvious but both women are thinking the same thoughts.

"What we do with him?"

Both Achara and Jo know if they let him free, he'll run to Bunnag and blab. They can't leave him in the boat. Contemplating their next move, Dek Lek sees a rag next to the pilot's seat, picks it up and takes a water bottle from her backpack and gestures toward the man with it. Jo nods.

"Get close enough to toss it to him Dek Lek. Don't go near him."

Dek Lek stops several steps from the man and holds up the water bottle and the rag with questioning eyes. Being naïve, she goes closer than she should after he nods his head affirmatively. When she is only a step away, and before Jo can react, he grabs Dek Lek and holds the knife to her throat, pulling her close to him as he rises off the seat. He's about to instruct the women to return him to shore when Jo moves with the swiftness of a gazelle. She can hit a bulls-eye with a pistol at fifty feet, every time. Stance, breathing, alignment is all automatic. Before he can finish his threat, a bullet enters his left eye and kills him. The man's body is thrown from the boat with a splash. The echo from the shot fades into silence of the bay. The knife clatters to the floor and Dek Lek falls beside it breaking into sobs.

"I… I'm sorry Jo. I'm sorry."

Jo bends to hold her close, sorry she had to witness the man's destruction.

"It's okay sweetie. He won't hurt anybody anymore."

Achara is standing over them. Jo's persona has just been polished to a higher sheen in her mind.

"You're good. That was a bitchin' shot. That settles the question of what we have to do with him. Look, tide's going out. He'll float outwards and if he doesn't sink or get eaten by the Reef sharks, the tide won't be back in until the middle of the night. We'll worry about it then. It was self-defense. There are two witnesses."

Jo and Dek Lek rise from the floor, with Jo keeping her close, moving stray hairs away from her forehead. The three of them move to the back of the craft and watch the man float, face down. The body bobs softly away from them. After a few moments. Jo directs Dek Lek to one of the seats and points to shore.

"Let's get back and tonight we find a way into that warehouse."

# CHAPTER 7

Achara and Jo, dressed in dark clothes, wearing skin-tight flexible gloves, slip in and out of the recesses of the buildings and the warehouse like shadows. Fifty feet from them, Dek Lek is in the front seat of Achara's SUV, doors locked. She has a disposable pre-paid phone Jo purchased earlier. There are two numbers on speed dial. One for Achara's cell, another for backup - a trusted friend who's on alert. It didn't take long for her to catch on when Jo was instructing her on its usage because her foster parents had one. She's perched on the edge of the seat where she can see the warehouse. She watches Jo and Achara disappear into the night. It's midnight plus ten.

The women approach the side door and pause. Jo has her back to the wall to the left of the door, Achara on the right. They listen. With a half-moon and intermittent clouds, the night dances between shades of bluish glow and total darkness. There are few streetlights in the industrial section. Late night people avoid this area. Jo speaks in a whisper.

"You hear anything?"

"Nothing. Try the door."

Jo furtively reaches out to try the knob. Locked, just what she expected. Feeling the front of the knob with her fingertip, she detects the slit where a key would be inserted, a single-entry system. She feels the door and finds no evidence of any other locks. Kneeling on the concrete step, she removes a pocket knife from a side pocket of her cargos. It's a one-hander with a thick, short blade, serrated edges. Flicking the blade open with her thumb, she feels along the door jamb with her left hand at knob level. She estimates the door stop is almost half an inch thick, about an inch-and-a-half wide. Wedging her knife under the wooden slat, she worries it up and down until she forces an opening from the jamb where she can push her knife through. The tip of the knife squeezes the edge of the striker and with a quiet snap, the door unlocks. Jo enters the darkness, Achara close behind.

Letting their night vision adjust, they see outlines of a workshop. Odors of oil and grease linger. The large garage door is not weather tight and a slither of light outlines its weakest edges. A transom, farther along the left wall, above a door, emits a faint flickering light, like a candle burning. Both women pull small penlights from their pockets. No windows can give them away from the street. Scanning the room, they verify its usage by the racks of tools, the workbench with a dented radiator on it, a hoist in the center of the floor with four greasy and oil-stained arms. On the far wall past the door on the left, a desk is piled with papers on one edge, a full in-box on the other and a laptop in the middle. The wall has a calendar of a girl in a flimsy swimsuit, a poster with one corner curled for lack of a pin of Evil Knievel jumping a bunch of buses, and a bulletin board full of sticky notes. They move to the door under the transom, one on each side and listen. Deep in the building, a drone is heard, a voice or voices, muffled by distance or walls.

"A TV", says Achara.

"Then it's safe to say we're not alone."

"I'd bet on it. Means they have something to protect."

"Or hide. Try the knob Achara."

It's solid, heavy duty. Holding her light close, she sees two deadbolts.

"We're not getting in this way."

They both look up at the same time. Jo turns to the desk and sees the chair in front. Four solid wooden legs but no back, more of a stool. Placing it at the foot of the door, she scurries up on it and peers through the transom window. It's dusty and smoke-stained limiting visibility. She can't see anything directly in front of her, the shadows are deep. In the distance is a window in some kind of enclosure. The TV is not visible. The flickering light of changing scenes illuminates the room but Jo can't discern anything from here. It's about twenty meters away she guesses. No one moves about. She cups the penlight in her palms and looks closely at the moulding surrounding the glass. She looks down at Achara and whispers.

"See if you can find me a flat screwdriver, the bigger the better."

She returns with a hefty tool a foot long and a wide blade for larger screws. Pushing the screwdriver under the moulding she pries it loose. The nails holding it are brads, sitting tightly in the wood for many years, and screech at their disturbance. In the stillness of the shop, it sounds like a banshee. Jo and Achara freeze. Five minutes go by before either move.

"That gave me a start. Be careful Jo."

"I know. These damn nails have been in there a long time."

A couple more nails protest as the moulding comes off. Jo passes each piece to Achara who places them on the floor to the side. When Jo removes the final piece of wood and turns to pass it and the screwdriver to Achara, she takes her hand off the glass. It's loose in the frame and the air pressure is greater in the warehouse. It falls inward, glances off Jo's shoulder and shatters when it hits the floor. Loudly.

A light goes on outside the enclosure, inside the warehouse. A clutter of machines is on the right and racks on the left. A walkway extends from this door to the back. Jo sees the partition goes all the way to the ceiling. Rough plywood makes a wall at the opposite end of the building. There is a door to the left of the window. It opens.

The man who emerges from the door is big for a Thai, large around the middle. A mop of unruly hair covers a round head. His moves are hesitant and sluggish. He's checking left and right. She can't make out facial features but the gun he holds as he advances toward them is clear enough. She alights from her perch, careful to not step on any glass.

"Shit. Quick put your light out."

"What Jo?"

"There's a man coming this way and he has a gun."

"Shit is right. Go to the left, I'll stay on this side if he comes in. I'll distract him, you take him out."

They move into position; Jo has her weapon drawn. Achara readies herself in a defensive position, hands loose, weight on the balls of her feet. They can hear footsteps approach and stop outside the door. They can hear the man breathing. The dead bolts snap open and the door slowly opens. No one moves. The man reaches in toward Achara to flip a light switch. She grabs his hand in both of hers and yanks forward. Caught off guard, the man rams head first into the door jamb, directly on the keeper of one of the deadbolts and it gashes his forehead. He yells out in pain. Not letting him recover, Jo steps from the edge and with both hands gripping her gun, she strikes him in the nape of the neck. He slams onto the floor.

Before they can recover, another man comes from the door and seeing Jo strike his companion, he kneels to shoot and hits the doorframe just a nick above Jo's head. She jerks back and Achara, drawing her weapon from a back holster, rolls out on the floor in a prone position and hits the man in the chest. The impact from the bullet leaves him sprawled on the floor. Both women remain still, Jo crouched by the door frame and Achara where she lies, gun pointing at the door. Nothing moves. Achara slowly rises and Jo meets her inside the warehouse. They find duct tape and rope, enough to immobilize and quell the first man. Heading toward the back, she waves Achara to follow.

"Let's go have a look."

Bypassing the body, they go through the doorway which opens into a large room, a set of stairs on the left. The ceiling is low. Rough plywood adorns the walls and ceiling. An old tube type TV sits on an empty wooden crate. A fridge, a counter with microwave, open cupboards with plates and glasses are along one wall. A well-used couch sits facing the TV, a couple of hard backed chairs are sitting by one side. An empty spool from heavy wire serves as a table covered with a couple of magazines, a half-eaten bag of potato chips and two near empty beer bottles. The room reeks of stale cigarette smoke and sweaty bodies. An open door in the back reveals a toilet and sink.

Something moves upstairs and the floor above squeaks. Jo puts her fingertip to her mouth and moves to the foot of the stairway. She signals Achara to watch the door into the warehouse.

Stepping on the sides of the treads close to the wall in case they're loose, she creeps upward. There is no door at the top, only an opening. No light. She can't see in but hopes to warn anyone watching and confuse them with English.

"I'm coming in."

Anyone unsure of what's coming through the door, and has a weapon, will be aiming at chest or stomach level, the largest mass. They won't be thinking at knee level. At least Jo hopes so when she plans on springing through the entryway. She's stunned when a voice calls out. Not what it says, nor that it's English but that it's the high-pitched voice of a child.

"There's no one in here except us."

A chill runs up Jo's spine.

"Are there lights in there?"

"The switch is inside on the left... no, I mean on your right."

Jo reaches in until she feels the square knob of a light switch and flips it open. She gasps when it exposes the room's contents. In a wire cage at the back of the room are a group of children. Mostly girls but a few boys. They cringe from the harsh lights and move to the back of the enclosure. The average age Jo guesses is ten years old but the bitter truth is some are as young as seven or eight. Most have disheveled hair and sleepy eyes, probably awakened by the gunshots. They are all dressed in the same style. Plain light blue cotton shifts that remind Jo of the garments hospitals use when you get undressed. The pens are framed with solid wood and chicken wire. A padlock holds the only door in place. The floors are filthy as are the legs, faces and hands of the children.

Tears well up in Jo's eyes when she stares at the youngest. A little girl with stubby fingers gripping the wires and eyes as big as a one-baht coin. They all look so lost. She can't believe what she's seeing. Stunned into silence, she watches the children move closer to the front to study her. Some have scratch marks and bruises on their faces, welts on their lower legs and one boy has a black eye. They have been punished for making too much noise or even talking so they are leery of the woman in front of them. Jo is interrupted by Achara who has moved to the bottom of the stairs and is curious of the quiet from upstairs.

"What is it Jo?"

Jo is afraid to speak, scared she might start crying. She pockets her gun and composes herself. Sticking her head out the doorway, she sees Achara at the foot of the stairs.

"Children Achara. Locked up."

"Can you get them out? We have to move. We can't stay here long."

Jo nods and returns to the room. The tallest child, maybe up to Jo's chest, is standing at the pen's locked door. She points to an old kitchen table in the opposite corner.

"The key is over there."

Jo looks among the debris on the table, a tray with several empty glasses and a pitcher of water, pliers and a couple of screwdrivers, children's books and an ugly weapon – a sap with blood on its edges. The key is on the tray. She grabs it and moves to the door. She speaks to the tall girl.

"We are going to get you out. Tell the others to be quiet and stay close together. We'll get you to safety. Remember, no noise. Ok?"

The girl nods and whispers to the other children in Thai. The little ones are jumping up and down with happiness until she scolds them to be still. Jo unlocks the door and hustles the children out and down the stairs to Achara who groups them outside the enclosure. There are eleven children. Jo wonders how they'll all fit in the SUV. She'll worry about that later. Now they need to get them away.

"Where are we taking them, Achara?"

"I've got an emergency number for Save the Children. They'll help. Right now, they look starved. We'll take them to my place, feed them, clean them up and find spots for them to sleep. It's not far from here."

The women hustle the children back through the garage. Clearing the broken glass out of the way, they go out through the door into the night and lead them in single file to the SUV. Dek Lek has dozed off with the phone in her hand and is woken by the clicking of the door lock. She is bewildered by the group of kids surrounding the vehicle until Jo opens the driver's door and tells her to help get the children in. The bigger ones get in first and move the smaller ones to their laps. Achara gets in the driver's seat, Jo has the two smallest on her knees. Dek Lek sits on the center console, chatting with the children, reassuring them that they are safe. The children are quiet, only speaking softly when Dek Lek asks them their names.

She pulls on Jo's sleeve to get her attention.

"What?"

Dek Lek points to the back, a girl curled up by one of the bigger kids.

"That's Malai"

Jo has a flash of the bikini bottom in the boat and looks at the innocent faces. She's fuming and has an idea.

"Wait Achara."

She opens her door and rearranges the children on the seat. Achara looks askance at her.

"Where you going?"

"It's better you don't know. I hate the son of a …" remembering the kids, "… the SOB… that did this. I'll slow him down a bit. I'll catch up to you at your place. Give me an hour or two. What's your address?"

Achara sees the grit in Jo's eyes and doubts she can convince her to stay put.

"Don't do anything stupid Jo. I'm only giving you an hour and if you're not at my place, I'm coming back."

"Thanks, Achara."

Achara gives her the street name and number, quick directions and the SUV pulls away and Jo melts into the darkness. She heads back to the warehouse. Unknown to her, an alarm has gone off on Bunnag's phone. He and the man with the eye patch are headed this way.

# CHAPTER 8

Jo races back to warehouse and circumnavigates the building taking note that it is separated from the other buildings on the side by at least ten meters. Entering the open door in the workshop, she uses her penlight to find the man they tied up earlier. Holding the light in his eyes she sees he's conscious and glaring at her. She pulls the gun from her waistband and holds it to his head. Reaching into her pocket she retrieves the knife and opens it with her thumb. Cutting the rope that binds his feet, she prods him to stand. He has to roll over to get his footing and as he does so, she watches him closely. When he's standing, she shines her pen light at the doorway and coaxes him toward it with the gun at his back. When they are outside, she backs off and pushes him forward. He's not stupid and understands. He takes off running.

Jo returns to the warehouse and unlocks an exterior door that leads to the wharf. Dragging the dead man with her hands under his arms, she pulls him out across the asphalt parking lot to the edge of the water where she dumps his body. Returning to the workshop she hunts for anything flammable. Under the rack of tools is a red jerry can. On the desk beside an ashtray is a lighter. Beside the laptop is a newspaper from which she removes several pages, folding them to fit a side pocket. Opening the cap of the can, she can smell gas fumes and notices that it is almost full, probably twenty liters or so. Hefting the can in both hands, she chucks the cap on the floor and begins to slosh the floors and fixtures with liquid. Leaving a trail into the warehouse, she pours more on the workbenches, the racks and finally on the wall of the enclosure. Chucking the can to the side she walks to the back door she dragged the body through. Using the pages from the newspaper and the lighter, she makes a small torch. When it's burning steady, she tosses it on the puddle where she finished emptying the jerry can.

A loud swoosh interrupts the quiet when the petroleum catches fire. It speeds through the trail she left behind, flames claiming every spot. The heat is intense and Jo rushes to the side door. She begins to creep along the side of the building toward the street. There is absolutely no light and it is hard to see. When she rounds the corner, she runs into the serious end of a pistol. It hits her in the forehead. And she collapses at the feet of the man with the eye patch.

# CHAPTER 9

When Achara stops at a red light a quarter kilometer from the warehouse, Dek Lek bolts from the car. Unable to stop her, Achara watches her run off back the way they came. Worried about the kids in the car, and with two of the little ones crying, she has to let her go. She'll get the kids home and call people she can depend on and hurry back. She shakes her head at having to deal with two reckless females but grins inwardly at their bravado.

By the time Dek Lek gets back to the warehouse, she sees Jo's limp body being lifted into the trunk of a big blue car. The warehouse has flames spurting from the back doorway and the metal siding is red hot in some places along the driveway side. Smoke curls into the sky, sparks float and scurry in the darkness like fireflies. She recognizes Bunnag, who has a phone to his ear and is silhouetted in the glare of the flames. Sirens can be heard in the background. Bunnag drops the phone in his pocket and is talking to the big man that placed Jo in the trunk. In the flickering light Dek Lek sees the eye patch. Not sure what to do, she goes to the car and opens the back door to crawl in and hunker down by the floor. The car is soon moving and Dek Lek is petrified.

They drive for less than five minutes when the car stops and Dek Lek can hear the conversation between the driver and whoever is outside. The voice from outside is formal and commanding. Eye Patch tells the person to contact Squadron Leader Simsek. A brief pause and the car starts moving. Slower now. From Dek Lek's position she can see streetlights and tall buildings. The car stops by one with a rounded dome. They wait in the stillness for several more minutes when she hears someone approach and blast Eye Patch.

"What are you doing here? And at this time of the night? You were only supposed to show up tomorrow night with the kids in the boat."

"The building is on fire. The kids are gone."

"What? What do you mean gone? We've already received upfront money for them. Who did this?"

Dek Lek hears the car door open and the driver get out.

"I can't answer those questions but I've got someone who can."

There's no sound for a moment and then Dek Lek hears the trunk being opened and a voice yell out. It's Jo.

"Help. Help me…"

Dek Lek cringes when she hears a slap, then Jo whimpering. Looking up at movement by the window, she sees the man with the eye patch leading Jo with his hand clamped over her mouth. The other man is issuing instructions and Dek Lek hears him until they move out of hearing range.

"Bring her in the hangar, through the back door. We'll use the lunch room, there's no one…"

Not certain what to do, Dek Lek peers over the car window. The area is deserted. Several large vehicles, trucks and odd shaped machines hide the car from the street. She can see the runway in front of the building with ground lights leading toward the water like candles at a vigil. She sees the two men and Jo disappear into a door at the rear.

She remembers the phone. Pulling it from her pocket, she pushes the #1 button and the little green phone icon. It rings several times until Achara answers, almost in a panic.

"Thank goodness you called. What's going on Dek Lek? Where's Jo?"

Dek Lek explains what has happened and where she thinks she is, a big building in front of wide road with lights on the side, not knowing the word for runway.

"Sounds like the Air Force base. Is the fat man with the moustache with them?"

"No, he stay at burning building. Only man with eye covered and another man. Name is Simsek. They have Jo in a big building here."

"What do you mean, burning building?"

"I think Jo set on fire."

"Oh shit. Ok. I can't get there for another half hour Dek Lek, maybe sooner but I'll have trouble getting in, and I don't know who I can trust there. I think I know the building you mean. Can you follow them?"

"Will try."

"Don't let them see you. Do you see the time on the phone, at the top? It should read 144 with two little dots between the 1 and the 4."

"Un-huh."

"When it reads 154, call me back if you can."

"Okay."

"Be careful."

Dek Lek replaces the phone in her pocket and opens the car door to get out. As the front door is open and the roof light is still on, she leaves it that way. Moving around the heavy machinery, she makes her way to the hangar door. It opens easily and without any noise. Moving slowly, she peeks in. She can't see much as the building is in darkness except for small rectangular windows facing the front, high up the wall. Light filters in but not enough to see the floor. She can make out the outline of a helicopter, the rotors glossy and reflecting the low light from the windows. She hears a commotion toward the back. There is another door slightly ajar and a light escapes the edge. She slithers along the wall until she is next to the door. One of the men talking in Thai and bad broken English.

"I don't understand what you're saying…"

Another slap and Jo is sobbing. Dek Lek doesn't know what to do. She already hates the men for hurting her friend. She has to stop them somehow. She moves to the other side of the door and follows a short wall where it cuts ninety degrees and moves toward the rear. The only other light is a large yellowish overhead one by the hangar door far to the front. It leaves a ghostly sheen near the back where there is a bench and tools hanging on a pegboard on the wall. Letting her eyes adjust, she sees what she needs. On the top of the bench is a variety of implements she doesn't recognize but there is a knife with a sliding blade and a tin cup containing a mixture of small nuts and bolts and a medium sized crowbar. Picking up the knife, she sees the thumb switch that moves the blade back and forth. She figures out how it works and slides it into her pocket. Gripping the tin cup in one hand and the crowbar in the other, she moves back to the edge of the room where the door is.

There are four large drums between the helicopter and the room. Crouching down by the side, she grips her weapon and tosses the cup toward the door she came in. All chatter in the room stops. She hears one of the men.

"Someone's out there. Go see."

The man with the eye patch furtively peeks out the door with a gun raised. Cautiously moving towards where he thought he heard the sound, he walks next to the drums and when Dek Lek sees the outline of his body, she swings the crowbar with all the might her small frame can muster. It connects with his tibia just below the knee and the crack is audible in the stillness. The prongs on the end of the crowbar, normally used to pull stubborn nails, rips into the skin of his calf muscle. A scream of pain fills the empty spaces and echoes off the walls. The heavy man goes to the floor. The gun rattles off into the darkness. Dek Lek scoots back behind the barrels and waits.

Squadron Leader Simsek is in a deep sweat. He's already nervous about his cohort and his captive being here. When he hears Eye Patch screaming, he panics and runs out with a drawn weapon. All he sees is the big man on the floor writhing in pain and moaning gibberish. He looks everywhere for any movement or people but can't see anything. He has to quiet the man before MPs come around. If he gets caught, it's not the Air Force command

41

he's worried about as much as Bunnag's thugs and superiors, cruel and merciless men. With the gun in a two-handed position he yells for Eye Patch to be quiet as he approaches him. In almost the same position as the man before, Dek Lek swings again. Only this time higher. The man is shorter and takes the full force of Dek Lek's swing in the crotch. Bending over in pain, he loses the gun. Dek Lek remembers Jo's action when the bad man was trying to pull her from her shack at the construction yard. High on adrenalin, she raises the crowbar and with the sharp prongs facing down, hits the man on the lower back, knocking him to the floor. She swings with all her might several times more. The prongs dig deep enough to sever the spinal cord and snap the backbone. If he survives, he'll never walk again. When she drops the crowbar to the floor, it clatters on the concrete. Standing over the men, she removes the knife from her pocket and slides out the blade.

Seeing them incapacitated, she runs back to the room where Jo is, finding her tied to a hard-back chair. Her face is bruised. Tears have made rills down her dusty face. Expecting Achara or another man, Jo is startled to see Dek Lek with a knife poised in her hand. A grin crosses her face.

"You're a real trooper Dek Lek."

"Trooper?"

"Never mind honey, cut me loose and let's get out of here."

Ten minutes later, the two of them are sneaking off the base. In the middle of the night, the guards at the entry are goofing off in the gatehouse and don't see them leave. Five minutes away, Achara meets them on the street. Rolling down the window, she gapes at the two of them.

"Whoa, what's going on here. How'd you get away?'

Jo pulls her young friend closer in a hug.

"My little hero here took on the bad guys and guess what? She won."

# CHAPTER 10

Eye Patch, a convicted felon, goes by the name of Pui, the nickname his grandfather gave him when he was a baby, a plump baby. His real name, the one used on his prison file and police records is Decha Kasemsarn. Suffering from a *nophthalmia* from birth, he was born with only one eye. Growing up in the slums of Bangkok, he was treated cruelly from the time he could walk. Like a dog that's been kicked around all its early life, he's mean and bitter. No one ever made fun of his eye or his eye patch more than once. He has a reputation for revenge, a murderous streak that leaves hapless victims in his wake. He fears no one. Except Bunnag.

He can't stay in the hangar. Biting through the pain, he drags himself to the barrels where Dek Lek was hiding. Pulling himself up onto his good leg, he feels the blood tricking from his torn calf muscle. It leaves a smeared trail along the concrete floor. Balancing himself on one foot he sees the crowbar lying beside Simsek. Wonders if he's dead. Doesn't care. Needs to flee.

Looking around in the dim light, he sees a pile of lumber across from him where it looks like shelves are being built. Mostly two by fours, he notices different lengths piled on top. Hopping on his good right leg, each bounce in agony, he crosses to the pile and leans down on it to fight the pain. One piece of wood is about four to five feet long. Standing straight, he picks it up and props it under his left arm, making a crutch. It digs into his underarm. The square edge is uncomfortable but it gives him some relief and balance. He heads out to the car.

Biting down, he overcomes the pain and pulls his leg into the car thankful it's not his right leg. He starts the car and heads toward the gate. Simsek got him in, there should be no trouble getting back out. Approaching the gatehouse, the guard checks who he is and waves him through. They don't see the sweat on his forehead, the grimace of pain on his face, the dark eye bent on revenge. Pui concentrates on the image of the woman and thinks of ways to hurt her. Later. He knows the woman helped the kids escape, Simsek got that much out of her. Right now, he needs to deal with Bunnag, who'll be fuming. He's not too worried, he's got something that might lead them to her.

He remembers patting her down, how much he liked the heft of her breast and the glare she gave him. They dumped the gun, penlight, phone and other junk from her pockets. He kept her wallet, a man's wallet, compact. Not much in it. Jo left her American express card and the forged passport in her room, hidden under the mattress. The only thing in the wallet is 15,000 Bhatt, which he pockets, Jo Delaney's driver's license and a post-it-note tucked in one sleeve with an address. A good place to start.

When he arrives at the warehouse, he finds it a collapsed heap. Leaping flames devour the aged wood. Smoke, dark and bilious from the tip of every flame, poisons the air above. A lazy breeze carries it off shore. Fire trucks, response vehicles, police cars all block the street for a half a kilometer. Competing lights, blue, red and amber rainbows flicker and circle in the night making it look like a party. Firemen are watering the next buildings to prevent spreading. People are gathered in knots, mesmerized by the burning building, the fire reflecting in their pupils. People hold their noses from the stink of hot plastics and lubricants afire.

Pui cruises slowly as far as yellow tape until a waist high barrier of roughly joined wood forces him to stop. He can see Bunnag in the light of the flames talking to a man in a uniform. He can't see what kind it is but as the hat looks official, it could be a fire chief. He needs to get his attention. Looking at a clot of people across the street at the edge of the barrier, a young boy, maybe thirteen or fourteen is staring at him, likely because of the eye patch. Thinking he's likely a street kid due to his shoddy clothes, Pui puts on his best fake smile and waves the boy over. Pui waves a one thousand baht note and points out Bunnag. Gives the boy a message.

Bunnag hustles to the car. With his baggy suit coat, tie pulled loose from its knot and neck unbuttoned, Bunnag looks as sloppy as usual. Sweat beads his upper lip. Pulling out a damp handkerchief to wipe his face, he gets in the car. He has to lift the two by four to make room.

"What is this for, your new enforcer?"

It's then Bunnag sees the pain on Pui's face as his leg throbs and swells and his boot is too tight.

"What's going on Pui? Where's the girl?"

"I got a busted leg. I think it's broke and a cut in the back. It hurts, man, hurts a lot, I need to get it fixed."

Bunnag's not thinking of the leg. The leg only tells him that something went wrong. His voice takes on a threatening tone.

"Where's the girl?"

Pui hangs his head on the steering wheel. Lies to save his skin.

"I don't know, she had help. We were attacked by several people in masks. I went down. So did Simsek. I think he's dead."

"What about the kids? They go in the fire?"

"No… no, she stole them away. We know that much. Like I said she had help. We couldn't get any more out of her before we were attacked."

Bunnag sits back, his head against the backrest considering his situation: his mechanic is missing, one of the watchmen was found dead on the wharf, the other gone or burnt in the fire. Simsek is out. The children are gone. The warehouse is gone. His number one thug is out of commission. The people he deals with will kill him. He has to get the kids back and deal with Pui. Looking over at his bodyguard, he decides to… He's interrupted by a grunt from Pui when he tries to straighten his leg. Pui feels the bad vibes from his boss. His use is limited now.

"Listen Bunnag, I have something. We find her; we find the kids. Look."

He stretches out his hand and passes Jo's wallet and her phone.

"We found these on her. Look at the yellow paper."

Bunnag takes the wallet. A man's fold over. Slim and easy to pocket. The post-it-note has an address. A short way south of there. Not far. Tucking it back in the wallet, he puts it in his suit coat pocket. He knows what he's going to do.

"Okay, let's get you fixed up. There's a doctor that owes me just down the coast. Can you slide over? I'll help you."

Groaning, Pui sidles to the passenger's seat and with the leg propped up and finds some relief. Bunnag takes the wheel and soon has them on the highway along the coast. Ten minutes later they're on a stretch of road that borders the water and a lagoon with scrub brush on the opposite side, no houses or buildings for almost a kilometer. He stops there, pulling to the side. Almost dawn, the grey edge on the horizon warns him he doesn't have much time. Traffic is sporadic. Before getting out, he disables the roof light.

"I need to take a piss."

Pui is in a daze, eyes closed. The rolling of the car almost lulled him to sleep but the steady throb in his leg keeps him awake. Bunnag stops at the rear of the car and opens the trunk. Under the rubber mat, in a sheath is a hunting knife. A seven-inch blade, unreasonably sharp. Bunnag moves around to the passenger side, facing the lagoon. Opening the door, Pui's head is only inches away. So is his chest. Bunnag leans in and with both hands plunges the knife right through the heart. Immediate cardiac arrest. Dead in less than fifteen seconds.

Bunnag looks both ways and seeing no vehicles approaching, he drags the heavy body from the car and removes the knife, wiping the blood off on Pui's shirt. He stopped his car where a path of sand leads to the lagoon through an opening in the bushes. Bunnag has to stop a couple of times to catch his breath. He finally gets the body to the edge of the lagoon and rolls it into the water. After giving it a shove with his foot, it bobs away like driftwood.

Back in the car, doors shut, blood cleaned up as best as he can, he studies the yellow paper once more. He knows where the street is. Pulling a U-turn, he heads north. The sun is a wink of bright red on the horizon. It will be daytime soon.

# CHAPTER 11

Achara is putting antiseptic and bandages on Jo's face where she was struck. A gash on one temple should have stitches but Jo refuses to go to a hospital and tells Achara to patch it up as best as she can. A black eye and swollen cheek make her a candidate for victim of the month. They're in the bathroom in the basement and Jo's sitting on the toilet bowl. She has on one of Achara's T-shirts. Hers, stained with blood, is in the garbage. Dek Lek is asleep on the floor in one of the bedrooms. Six kids are asleep in various rooms in the house. The other five are at Achara's neighbour's, a retired couple from Germany. No questions asked, they've learnt to trust Achara. Putting the last strip of tape on the bandage on her temple, Achara backs off and points to the mirror over the vanity.

"Have a look. Don't enter any beauty contests for a while."

They laugh and Jo moans.

"Don't make me laugh, it hurts my cheek."

Eyeing her image, she cringes at the sight. The eye turning bluish black around the edges. The rawness on the puffed-up cheek and the gauze on her temple.

"Yikes! Yeah, I've looked better.

"How you feeling?

"Headaches going away thanks to the Advil. I just want to sit down for a minute and I need a coffee."

They go upstairs and check the kitchen; an island in the center of the floor, three bar stools at the high side backing onto the living room, the back door and hallway to the bedrooms on the right. Jo pulls a stool back and crawls up. Achara makes coffee and readies their cups.

"You want to talk about it, Jo? Don't know if it was a good idea starting that fire. Bunnag's not going to like that and with his kids missing, he'll be hunting for heads. They know what you look like."

Jo clasps her hands in front of her. She's leaning ahead, elbows on the counter, watching Achara fuss around the kitchen. She inhales the aroma of ground coffee beans.

"I was so angry, Achara. All I could see was that bikini bottom of that little helpless girl floating in the dirty water in the boat. How could men be so cruel? I wanted to put him out of commission, do something to hurt him."

"Well, he's got men missing, the kids missing, his warehouse gone. I'd say we did some damage."

She interrupts the bubbling of the percolator to pour two mugs full. Sliding one across, she keeps hers in both hands, blowing on the rising steam, looking at Jo across from her.

"Black okay?"

"Sure."

"What are you going to do now Jo? They have your wallet. They know where you live. You can't go back there."

Jo stares at her mug of coffee. Deep in thought. How would she handle this if she were still a cop? She'd get the bastard.

"We'll go after him. We know there's a connection at the base. When we left, the man in the uniform was lying on the floor. I don't know if he was dead or unconscious. Dek Lek says she hit him on the back four times with a crowbar. You said you have contacts there; something will have to come up."

Achara is waving her hands, backing off.

"Whoa now. I'm not taking on the Air Force. You hired me to find the girl. We did that. You're paid up for another day but I'm not going that route. Un-uh! And I'm putting that gun I gave you on the expense sheet."

Jo looks up.

"Yeah, I'm good for it."

She's forgotten to ask what is happening with the kids.

"What about the Save the Children?"

"Two volunteers brought clothes and some extra food right away. Later this morning they're coming to pick them up, get them sorted out and returned to their homes. I thought you would want to return Preeda's daughter yourself."

"Yes, that would feel good. Thanks Achara. Something decent is coming out of this mess."

Sipping on their drinks, they consider their next move. Jo frowns at her thought.

"I have to go back to the cottage. I have personal things I can't leave behind."

Achara looks out toward the living room window, which faces east. Above the tree line of her neighbour's place, morning is dawning in a pink halo.

"If you're going, we'd better go soon."

Checking the digital clock on the stove, Jo sees it's almost 6 a.m. Nodding her head in agreement, she sits back and finishes her coffee. Achara holds her finger up to indicate waiting for a moment. She leaves the room for five minutes and returns with a handgun. She passes it to Jo who looks at it with raised brows.

"How many of those things do you have?"

"Enough."

Jo tucks it in her waistband.

"Let's wake Dek Lek and the oldest girl to warn them and keep an eye on the rest. They can get the kids fed when they get up if we're not back right away. It shouldn't take us long."

\*

When the women drive up to Jo's place, they scan the area for cars parked near or anything odd. Stopping fifty meters away, they watch the house. Bunnag is watching them with binoculars from across the street. He parked his car at the back entrance to a grocery store and is hidden in an alley next to it, behind several dumpsters. When he sees two women emerge from the vehicle, he recognizes Achara, having butted heads during her investigation. He grits his teeth thinking he should've taken her out back then. The other woman is the one that left him naked in the construction yard. The veins in his neck throb, and he's frothing by the time they disappear around the building to the front.

He drops the binoculars on the ground and checks for the gun in his waistband and the knife in his pocket. Realizing he'll have to be careful, he takes note of employees arriving at the stores along this side of the street and other people moving about their cottages. The traffic is picking up, delivery trucks, mopeds and cars racing for space and time. Eyeing their vehicles, he smiles to himself. He only needs one of them. The others he'll kill.

# CHAPTER 12

They took Jo's keys, so she has to break in. Smashing a glass pane in the door, she reaches in and flips the deadbolt. Achara tells her she'll stay outside and watch the building. As there's enough light from the east, Jo doesn't need to turn the light on. Rushing into the bedroom, she grabs her carry-on. Looking for her things, she wants to stuff a couple changes of clothes, her diary, the things she hid under the mattress, and the same with Dek Lek's backpack. Finishing her packing, she runs into the other bedroom.

Achara is circling the cottage, eyes everywhere. Going around the back of the house, which faces the street, she doesn't see Bunnag who is hiding behind her vehicle. She scans the perimeter and moves slowly toward the beach and the front of the cottage. Bunnag's having second thoughts about trying to subdue the women here. He's not familiar with the layout, doesn't like the dark-skinned woman doing sentry duty. Too risky. Too many people around. He decides it might be best to follow them and hopefully it'll lead him to the kids and payday. He'll need backup.

What he fears worse is that he needs to contact Group Captain Wattana, one of the masterminds behind the child abduction scheme. Wattana is the middle man for the children, Bunnag only the collector. He was supposed to deliver the children to the base by boat later today where Wattana and Simsek would take over. Bunnag has no idea how the men smuggle the children out or where they take them. He suspects it's to a ship or boat offshore but he's only guessing. He doesn't care. The $2000.00 US dollars per child is all the motivation he needs. He already received $20,000.00 for this bunch. Trouble is most of that money is gone. He has to get the children back. Otherwise, he's a dead man.

Rushing back to his vehicle, he retrieves his binoculars first and parks his car twenty meters behind Achara's SUV. His car is out of sight behind two other vehicles. He waits. Ten minutes later the women return to Achara's vehicle and leave. He moves into traffic several cars behind and watches where they go, following discretely.

It doesn't take long for them to reach Achara's house. With the sun barely over the treetops behind them, two of the children are sitting on the front steps in long shadows eating cereal from bowls. They run to meet Achara and Jo when they get out of the car. They're chirping like birds freed from their cage, all aglow from being out of the pen and going home. The little boy hugs Achara, following her to the neighbour's house to inform them of the plans by Save the Children. The girl is following Jo into the house just as Bunnag drives by, noting the number on the house. He pulls into a convenience store up the street and parks in a space facing Achara's place. Hitting speed dial, someone answers on the second ring. Bunnag tells them where he is.

"… and bring Prawat with you. Come armed."

Knowing they won't arrive for another ten minutes, he goes into the store to use the washroom. Jo greets Dek Lek, commending her on her help.

"Thanks, Dek Lek. I'm really depending on you to keep an eye on them for us. This isn't over yet."

"Are there still some bad men looking for us?"

"I think so and until we get the kids to their homes, we have to watch out. Take the little ones downstairs and get them to watch some cartoons or something. The Save the Children people will be here in a couple of hours and then we'll decide what we're going to do. Okay?"

Dek Lek runs off to gather the older girl and the others to the basement. Achara returns and sends the boy downstairs with them. When everyone is out of earshot, Achara meets Jo in the kitchen where she is making more coffee.

"Jo, I think we might have trouble."

Jo stops and faces Achara.

"What's going on?"

"On the way back from my neighbours, I think I saw the car that was at the wharf yesterday when we sailed past the warehouse, the big old Mercedes. There's one parked at the store up the street just like it and it's too coincidental. We must've been followed."

"If that's the case, they're coming for the kids."

"And likely for us."

"That too. I think this is what we should do."

Jo and Achara form a plan. The first thing they do is warn the kids. Moving them to the utility room, they have them hunker down under the stairway. One of the children senses danger and starts to cry. Dek Lek takes her into her arms and gives her one of the lollipops Achara gave them. A stern warning to all of them by Achara tells them to be absolutely quiet if they want to get back to their homes again, as well as to not come out until either her or Jo says it's ok.

Moving back upstairs, Jo positions herself by the front window, crouching low enough to not be seen but with an eye open to the front of the building. She has the gun Achara gave her and a baseball bat. Achara is in the same position in a rear bedroom. The back yard is short, bordered by a small tool shed, and a hedge of mature bamboo almost five meters tall. A sidewalk and a street are beyond. She too has her gun out and a poly-carbonate side-handle baton. Twenty-four inches long, it has a side handle six inches from one end. Achara has had it for ten years and is adept in its usage. They wait.

Only for six minutes. Advancing to the front door is a young woman. She carries a briefcase. She's wearing a light white linen pant suit with a pink shirt. She carries in one hand what Jo thinks is a business card. Jo curses at the untimely visit. Too early for someone selling Avon, or insurance, it's probably someone from Save the Children.

"We've got company Achara. A lady. Hurry, come trade places with me."

The women switch positions when the doorbell rings. Achara, peeks through the peephole in the door. The woman is small in stature, common amongst Thai women. A smile splits her plain face, seemingly harmless. Achara knows it's not Jehovah Witness as they all come in pairs. Eyeing the surrounding street, she doesn't see any threats. Flipping the lock, she opens the door, her gun in hand behind her back. The baton is near on a side table.

The woman greets Achara telling her she is with the Red Cross and it has come to her attention that there may be children here that need help. Achara relaxes slightly. She's dealt with the Red Cross before. She opens the door to admit her. When the lady walks by, her head down, Achara doesn't like the way she reads. There is a scar along the woman's chin, a skull tattooed on the neck and eyes guarded and dark. The woman steps into the foyer, scans the living room and while her back is turned, Achara pulls her gun out, points it at her head and slams the door shut.

The noise causes the woman to react by turning sharply to find the gun facing her. With lightning speed, a hardened fist comes up to knock the gun away, followed by a kick to the ribs that drives Achara back against the side table, scattering photos and candles to the floor. The woman readies herself to strike again. Achara grabs the baton and deflects the jab aimed at her throat. Before the woman can react, Achara swings the baton on the side handle and whacks the woman on the thigh. Grasping her leg with pain, she tumbles to the living room floor. In her downward arc, she fumbles for a knife attached to her ankle. Achara catches the movement and steps in with the baton straight out to strike the dagger from the woman's hand, breaking two of the fingers.

Jo hears the scrambling of the photos and glass containers but before she can help Achara, she sees something in the bamboo trees, a disturbance. She pauses but nothing moves. A scream draws her to the living room. Rushing from the hallway, she goes by the back door. When she's in front of the door, the glass on the upper half bursts into a hundred shards. The bullet glazes her right shoulder muscle, burning away the cotton fabric and two layers of skin. Jo bites down on the pain and throws herself behind the kitchen island. She can see Achara hovering over the woman, ready to strike. The bullet startles everyone. The woman takes advantage of Achara's hesitation and lashes out with the heel of her boot, striking Achara in the chest.

The back door bangs open, slamming into the wall. A bull of a man comes roaring through. The door gave easier than he anticipated and he is thrown off balance. Wishing she'd hung on to the baseball bat, Jo leaps from the behind the island, the man three steps away. Intending to go for the throat, she spins to strike him with her heel. He tries to sidestep the blow but it strikes him in the ribs, cracking two of them. The force drives him back against the wall. Jo is relentless. She steps in to hit him on the rebound. She strikes him in the nose with her fist. Staring at her with bleary eyes and a bleeding nose, he grabs her in a bear hug, crushing her chest. She hits him in the nose again with her forehead and stomps on his toes. He grunts and reaches up to protect his nose. Turning quickly, she attempts to knee him in the groin but he swipes her foot aside and knocks her off balance, while drawing a pistol from a shoulder holster. Jo sees the glint of the metal of the barrel and letting herself fall, pulls her gun from her waistband. Before he can react, she puts a slug into his chest cavity. He's dead before he hits the floor.

Achara is driven into the side table again and the woman is righting herself to attack with a pistol drawn. Swiveling into a prone position, Jo places a nine-millimeter hole in the woman's head just above the ear. Bone and brain matter cover the wall where the bullet lodges into the wall. The woman's lifeless body falls on the coffee table. The blast provokes the children to start screaming, terrified by the commotion above.

Jo rushes to the back door and sweeps the yard with her gun. Achara takes the front, both looking for more adversaries. Bunnag has been watching, waiting for a signal. When he sees Achara in the yard, he knows his people have been put out of commission. Cursing, he's unsure what to do next. Seeing no other threats, the women go back inside and Jo tends to the children. Once the children are calmed down, Jo warns them to stay put and returns to the kitchen, shaking from the adrenaline rush. The searing pain on her back reminds her of her injury. Achara looks at the wound.

"You're lucky. The bullet made a three-inch line across the muscle in your back. It needs to be dressed. There's not any blood. The bullet must've sealed off the blood vessels like a burn."

Jo points at the man.

"What are we going to do about these two?"

"Before we do anything, I need to thank you. I know words aren't enough but I owe you big time. About these two, we have no choice now; we need to call in the police. We…"

The large picture window in the front explodes inward from a gunshot at the front of the house. Both women crouch down and Jo crawls forward to peer out the front door window. Bunnag is standing on the street, pointing a gun at the house. He stands by the open door of his car. Seeing a silhouette behind the door window he aims and takes several shots. One blasts the glass, the others lodge in the steel door. Jo reacts quickly and fires wildly back through the shredded glass. It's all the priming Bunnag needs to leave. He gets back in the car. Jo stands and aims at the driver but with the car running, Bunnag makes his escape. But not before Jo puts a bullet in the rear tire. The car swerves and slues but Bunnag straightens it out and floors it, ruptured tire and all. Jo races into the kitchen and grabs Achara's keys from the counter.

"Look after things Achara, I'm going after him."

"No, wait for me…"

Jo's not listening. Hoping Bunnag will be slowed down by the flat tire, she runs to the SUV and tears from the yard. Bunnag can't be far ahead. All she sees is red. Anger clouds her mind. The only image that remains clear is the bikini bottom in the boat.

# CHAPTER 13

Jo catches up to the old Mercedes abandoned on the side of the road. Bunnag is pulling a young woman from the driver's seat of a Volkswagen Jetta. She falls to the street, yelling and shaking her fist at Bunnag who is heading off with her car. When Jo slows to avoid hitting the girl, she sees someone has stopped to help so she pulls quickly around them. Bunnag cuts in and out of traffic. He turns right at a busy intersection, cutting a scooter off. and takes the main street that follows the beach. She's almost on his tail when a hand appears from the driver's window with a gun pointed in her direction. The first two go wild, but the third enters the grille and steam from the punctured radiator momentarily obscures Jo's vision. She almost misses him turning toward the air base. Jo is a hundred meters from the entrance when the SUV overheats and stalls. Pulling over, she runs ahead only to see Bunnag gain entrance and head into the base.

Bending over to catch her breath, Jo's weariness is evident by a heavy sigh. She knows this should be left in the police's hands. What worries her is that if someone higher up in the Air Force is involved, and they've been getting away with what they're doing, too many palms are getting greased. Not knowing how the system works here, she's heard too many rumours about bad cops. She needs to get on the base, hunt Bunnag down and subdue him... or put him out of business.

She edges her way along the perimeter fence festooned thickly with ivy by the entrance to the base where the men in the guardhouse can't see her. Looking for a way in, she thinks she might be able to enter from the beach side but that'll take too long. Hidden from prying eyes, she studies her watch as the minutes tick by, waiting for an opportunity to move. Uncertain of what to do, she hesitates until a solution to her problem shows up.

*

In the interim, the last half hour Bunnag has been sitting on an uncomfortable couch outside Group Captain Wattana's office. His rumpled shirt, loose tie and oily skin make the secretary regard him with obvious distaste. A *Visitor* tag hangs from the lapel pocket of his suit coat. He's nervous, fumbling with an elastic band he keeps twisting around his fingers, and staring at the floor. One foot keeps time to an unknown rhythm. He waits another unbearable fifteen minutes until the darkly stained door opens and a young officer leaves. The secretary's intercom buzzes and she points Bunnag to the door.

Group Captain Wattana's persona is one of order. Hair neatly combed, fresh shaven face, smooth skin, high cheekbones and unwrinkled uniform. Only the eyes are shadowed. He speaks with the authority invested in him. He's not happy.

"I told you to never come here Bunnag. This better be good."

They're standing in the middle of the room to the right of the desk by the trophy wall. Bunnag is wringing his hands. He is not scared of many people but Wattana frightens him. Too many hard edges and no compassion.

"I had no choice. The children… are gone."

Wattana was expecting this, having supervised cleanup of the Simsek mess earlier but had hopes it wasn't so. He turns his back to Bunnag with his hands joined behind his back and walks to the large window behind his desk, staring at something on the horizon as he talks.

"You fool. I don't know how much longer I can contain this. I understand your warehouse is still smoldering?"

Bunnag clinches at the thought.

"Yes."

"What was Simsek doing at the hangar last night and who hit him? He may not recover."

"He and one of my associates were questioning the woman that we believe set the fire and stole the kids away. They were supposed to get her to tell them where the children were. But she escaped."

"And what of your… associate?"

Bunnag remans silent. Wattana turns to study Bunnag's hesitation. He can read the look on his face.

"Good. One less thing to worry about. Now why are you here?"

Wiping his brow with a rumpled handkerchief, Bunnag explains what took place earlier this morning. His call for back up. The unfortunate results. His narrow escape. His frustration.

"I don't know what to do. My manpower has been depleted. I need your help."

"Were you followed?"

Bunnag had hoped to omit this part.

"Yes. Only to the gatehouse. The woman that escaped was pursuing me. I disabled her vehicle and came here. I need you to help me settle this. We need to find her, establish who else is helping her and do something. They may either still have the goods or are moving them now."

Wattana raises his brows, rubs his chin – a habit when he's thinking.

"It's possible. The police will be there now I expect. Who is this woman? And how can one woman be such a nuisance?"

Bunnag produces Jo's wallet and passes it to Wattana.

"Caucasian. Canadian. Unsure of any particulars."

Wattana waves to a seat in front of his desk.

"Sit down and give me a minute."

Sitting at his desk, Wattana calls up a search engine on his computer. Keys in Jo Delany. There's too many of them and none that look like her photo on her Canadian driver's license.

"A Canadian? What would she be doing here? Where is this house you sent your people?"

He gives Wattana the address, which he jots down on a notepad.

"What about the police?"

Wattana waves it off without taking his eyes off the computer screen.

"Never mind the police. Once it's linked to missing children, Saetang will use his influence as chief to divert it from us. But now we must concentrate on the woman. Hopefully the children are still in hiding somewhere."

"And if they're not?"

"Then you are in very big trouble Bunnag. In fact, you are already in trouble. I was supposed to have those children delivered tonight. There is a very small window of opportunity. Unless we find them quickly, you will be the one to suffer the consequences Bunnag. Not me. Now be quiet and let me think."

Bunnag's adams apple bobs uncontrollably, his mouth goes dry and hate fills his eyes. Although he still carries his gun, he has no ammo left, no extra magazines. If he had, he'd kill Wattana now and run. He has no choice but to wait. Wattana on the other hand considers Bunnag a liability. He has the address and description of the woman. It's time for him to call in his contact, someone off base that shares the profits, someone who stands to lose as much as him. One with no conscious, a stone heart. He decides his next move. He scribbles something on a smaller notepad, tears the top sheet off and passes it to Bunnag.

"I have one more appointment I must attend. I will be free in an hour. Wait for me in your vehicle in the parking lot and I will come for you. Park in the rear. Take this and if anyone bothers you, show it to them. They'll leave you undisturbed. Now get out of here."

# CHAPTER 14

A utility truck pulls in behind two other vehicles, waiting to be allowed in. The back deck has large spools of wire, a workbench, tools boxes and a cherry picker. Two textured metal steps provide a way in. When the guard moves to the driver's door and out of vision, Jo rushes to the back and throws herself in behind one of the heavy spools. The guard does a quick check, sees nothing strange and the truck moves into the base. Jo can't see where it's going but it moves about for several minutes. She can hear the drone of a jet engine, the banging of metal on metal like something being hammered, the voices of men and women at work. The odor of burning kerosene can't mask the scent of brine. She knows she's close to the water. When the truck stops, she jumps from the back of the truck and runs toward the nearest building. Taking cover beside a pile of used tires, she scans the grounds.

She is beside a repair shed when the truck stops. Across a parade ground, there is a military museum and several residences a good distance away, standing by themselves on a dead-end street. Long, green lawns in the back lead to the water's edge. She assumes them to be for the commander and other senior officers. She tries to pay attention to the streets they were on by peeking over the spool. They seem to be on a main thoroughfare. Mostly administrative type buildings, parking lots, a water tower, fire station, some apartments and quite a few side streets. Bunnag could be anywhere. He'd have to be in one of the admin buildings or more likely at an arranged spot. Now she's near the industrial part and the hangars, close to the water. There are many civilians on base. It's too big to look everywhere.

Uncertain and frustrated, she decides to comb the hangar area where she was held captive but when she gets there, too much commotion forces her away. People were cleaning up the aftereffects of Dek Lek's temper and stealth. Returning to the repair shed, she sees two cars approach the farthest residence on the right, stopping in the driveway. The first one to pull in is a

58

Volkswagen Jetta. Both drivers get out, one is uniformed, the other is Bunnag. The very sight of him causes her blood pressure to go up.

She's keen enough to know that whoever the uniformed man is, this is the connection they're looking for. She needs to get in the house. It's a hundred meters in the open and another to the last house, she estimates. There are too many people moving about. Not sure how she can get skirt the parade ground and the street along the houses, she's disturbed by a door opening behind her. Crouching down behind the tires she watches a man leave a side door. He's dressed in oil-stained coveralls and doesn't wear a hat. Not sure if he's a civilian or not, she has a flash of how she might maneuver around the base.

When he moves out of sight, she speed dials Achara. No answer but the answering service kicks in. Jo explains quickly where she is and what she plans on doing. She creeps to the side door and cautiously opens it. Inside she can see several doors on the left and an open work area on the right where several vehicles are being repaired. One is up on a hoist and the other two are being serviced by men bent over the open hoods. Stepping in, she looks around for cover. Just then, a man enters the work area from one of the side doors, buttoning up a new pair of coveralls. When he's out of range, she edges toward the door and peers through a window into the room. It is a locker room and has a rack of coveralls hanging at the back, all in plastic coverings like drycleaners provide. Seeing no one around, she enters and hastily looks for her size. After donning a pair, she steals a side cap with two buttons on the front and places it low on her brow. Not sure how she looks she figures it'll have to do. One of the workers notices her when she exits the room but with her disguise, he pays her no attention. Picking up a small toolbox from a nearby bench, she leaves the building and heads toward the house. She still has her gun.

She doesn't know what rank the insignia on the side hat she is wearing but the few airmen driving by in jeeps or walking salute her. She keeps her head down. The driveway beside the house where she's heading doesn't have any cars parked there so she takes a chance no one is inside and steals around the back. Staying close, she has her back to the wall as she creeps closer. Sparkles on the water from the glaring sun catches her eye. She scans the water for any other threats. There is a large ship anchored several hundred meters off shore and dinghies are moving back and forth, repairs being made to the exterior aft section. No one else near.

When she reaches the target house, she hears loud voices, an argument. There is a two-level deck in the back. A patio door on the upper level reveals a dining area and part of the kitchen. The voices, high pitched, full of anger, seem to be coming from the basement. She sees a back door at ground level. Assuming it's an entrance to the basement, she sidles around the deck and when she reaches for the doorknob to try it, she's startled by a gunshot from within. It's not a loud retort, muffled by the walls. She's thinking small caliber gun maybe a 22. Dropping down by yew shrubs, the soil under her feet spongy, she waits in the silence that follows.

Several minutes pass until she hears someone leaving from a side door. Where she is she can peek around the edge of the house toward the driveway and sees the uniformed man running to his car and leaving. It doesn't bode well for Bunnag. Unsure if there is anyone else in the house, she waits twenty minutes before climbing the five steps to a small landing in front of the door. There's an opaque window in the upper portion of the door that she can't see through. Trying the knob, she finds it unlocked, the man forgetting in his haste perhaps… or on purpose. Glancing around to see if anyone is watching, she sees no one. No sirens wailing. No-one rushing to follow up. She enters the house.

The entryway faces a set of stairs leading to the basement. To the right, one step up is the kitchen. Unsure if she's alone, she draws her weapon and calls out.

"Anyone here?"

Silence. Remembering where the voices seemed to be coming from, she advances down the stairs. At the bottom, it opens to a large rec room with a wide-screen TV on the far wall, two leather couches, a chrome and slate coffee table with an overturned vase. Two narrow windows on the top portion let in the only light. It reveals shadows sitting in the corners, a bookcase, and a multi-shaded area rug with a dead body on it. A red stain in the center of his white shirt is turning crimson. Bunnag is dead.

Lowering her weapon, she stands over the corpse. Several magazines lie scattered near the body, likely knocked from the table when he fell. One of them lies open on his head, the pages squished on his untroubled brow. She kicks it aside. The eyes stare blankly up at the ceiling. Normally she feels some compassion for a dead person. But not this one.

Contemplating her next move, she wonders again how high up this goes. She hoped it ended with Bunnag but her hate still boils. Remembering Achara's words, 'We can't take on the Air Force', she decides she can't do any more. If the local police can't move on this, then it's time to go higher up in the Royal Thai Police. She replaces her pistol in her overalls pocket and decides to get as far away as possible.

She's on the second step when a man shaped shadow fills the window in the door and the doorknob turns.

# CHAPTER 15

After Jo left, Achara hustles the children away to the neighbours and deals with Save The Children representatives that came to collect them. The neighbouring couple offers to watch Malai and Dek Lek. Then she calls her contact, Lance Corporal Li. When he arrives, she doesn't mention anything about Jo or the burnt warehouse. She tells him she received an anonymous call about abducted children and where they could be found. She goes on to claim she doesn't know who these intruders were but says that they must have something to do with the kids. There is no choice but to inform his superiors.

They grilled Achara, going over the events, with a detective and the chief himself who arrives a half-hour after the first patrol car. She finds it odd that he should be there but he brushes her off when she asks why. He checks her cell phone for the mysterious message, and who called, but she tells them it came in as a private number, no digits showing. Knowing it would not be a good time to be disturbed, she switches it to vibrate before she puts it back in her pocket. If they do check her records, a private number called yesterday but it was a government office responding to her call about her license renewal. They question the neighbours and the convenience store clerk only to confirm there were many gunshots. But no one saw anything. Bunnag's car was impounded. A young lady made a report her car was stolen by a man fitting the description of Bunnag. She didn't see where it went. It all helped in Achar's claim of self-defense.

With Li's assurance of Achara's trustworthiness, both he and Achara are told in an official manner to make themselves scarce. Li was told to resume his regular duties. The police have Achara's house taped off. She has been warned not to leave the city and to let the police know where she is staying. She will be contacted when it is time for her to return to her house. Before they leave, her phone vibrates. Even though it could be Jo, she doesn't answer. Too many people around.

They keep her gun. She's not sure what she will do if ballistics show that it wasn't her gun that killed the two intruders. Shrugging it off, she starts walking away from the house. Unsure of her next move and with no vehicle, Li offers her a lift.

"Where to Achara?"

She's not listening.

"You know this will get covered up."

"What did you expect?"

"This has to stop."

Li shakes his head. He's not a big man, just shy of 168 centimeters, a little shorter than her. His round face is a mask of frustration.

"Listen Achara. I've already been warned off of this. I don't have any authority. I will sacrifice everything I've worked for if I stick my nose in any deeper. I do a lot of good police work. I make a difference but I can't fight this. It's worse for you. You're not out of suspicion yet. You make a stink and you'll be doing time."

Achara rests her head back against the headrest, eyes closed, thinking. She's about to say something when she remembers the phone vibrating a few minutes ago.

Achara listens to the fifteen-second conversation with mouth agape. Turning to Lance Corporal Li, she drops her voice.

"Can you get us into the air base?"

"The air base?"

"I don't have time to explain everything but I lied. I found them with an accomplice. The kidnappers are tied to someone on the base."

"If you knew this, why didn't you contact me?"

"You know why. We've been through this before. Whenever complaints are filed over missing children, they get lost somewhere in the administrative bullshit."

"Who's this accomplice?"

"She's not a resident. She's a visitor to our country. A good woman. I didn't want to get her involved."

"Why the base now? Was that her on the phone?"

"She's on the base with a dead body and someone coming to get her.

# CHAPTER 16

Hidden in a closet on the basement level, Jo hears someone entering the house. Quiet as the shoes lined up in front of her, she's sitting on her heels, back against the wall, uncomfortable but ready to spring up. Her gun points forward. With a hefty gulp, she realizes that she only has one bullet left.

Footsteps on the tiled floor get louder. Jo calms her breathing, steadies her nerves. Listening carefully, she hears the sounds stop, carpet on the stairs. The middle steps are squeaky. The squeaks end abruptly. The closet is to the left of the stairs in a short hallway. It's close enough that Jo can hear the sound of someone breathing. Whoever it is, has just seen the dead body. Jo hears the slow slide of a gun from its leather holster, its whisper an ominous sound. The steps are now at the bottom of the stairs. The noon sunlight streams into the windows, a sliver of it outlines the bottom of the closet door. A pair of feet now blocks out the light. And the door is yanked open.

Jo hunches up her shoulder when she springs from the base of the closet. She rams the man directly in the stomach, knocking the gun he holds from his hand. The momentum of Jo's thrust drives the intruder into the short wall, knocking a framed photo off its hook. Her hat flies off. Gasping for breath a man falls to the floor. Jo backs off, startled by who it is. It's impossible!

Adam Thorne staggers up, straightens his sport coat and grins at Jo who is gaping, bug eyed, stunned into silence, at her former partner from Canada.

"Can't you stay out of trouble Naylor?"

# CHAPTER 17

Jo has both hands on her face. She thinks she's hallucinating.

"It can't be you! What… what are you doing here Adam?"

He gives a closed mouth smile, hands open, palms up.

"Aren't you glad to see me?"

A forgotten sense of safety with Thorne at her back returns as she remembers all the tough spots they've been through. She softens up, rushing to embrace him in a hug.

"Yes, yes I am. I can always depend on you, partner."

She backs off and he holds her forearms in his hands, looking directly in her eyes.

"Oh Jo, look at your pretty face. You know, a black eye doesn't become you. I hate to see what's under that bandage on your forehead."

"Never mind me, let me tell you…"

He puts a finger to her lips.

"I know what's going on. I know what's at stake. I'll explain everything but we need to get out of here. Whoever killed your friend here, is coming back for the body and I expect that will be soon."

He grabs her hand and tows her up the stairs.

"You have a car Adam?"

"No, I had to come in by foot. It's quite a distance. Took me fifteen minutes."

Before they exit, he pulls out two visitor tags and gives her one. Blue clip-ons, printed with big white characters in Thai and English. She tags it on the waist band of her slacks.

"Compliments of a Lance Corporal Li, a friend of Ms. Jones."

Jo looks at him with a puzzled frown.

"And where'd you get the gun?"

"Never mind that, I'll fill you in soon. Achara's waiting for us at the guardhouse parking lot."

Opening the door, he peeks out and quickly pulls his head back in. Gritting his teeth, he holds the door with his back.

"Damn!"

"What is it Adam?"

"A van is backing into the driveway, looks like an ambulance, sort of. Something from the base. They must be coming for the body. Quick, into the basement. Back in the closet."

"What about you Adam?"

They are at the bottom of the stairs. Beyond the closet is another door. Pointing for Jo to crouch down, he does a fast look for where the door goes. A utility room.

"I'll hide in here."

Two men enter, jabbering in Thai and laughing at some joke. They're not being discrete. Heavy boots clomp about. Silence for fifteen seconds when they get to the bottom, brief fascination of a dead body. The louder of the voices seems to be in charge shouting out commands. Both voices are raised in what seems to be an argument, then silence.

The smaller of the two men sent to pick up the body, is a kleptomaniac. Worse than a crow. The smaller and the shinier, the better.

"*Changtongkandurop.*" (I want to look around.)

"*Reo!*" (Be quick!)

Jo and Adam hear him walk about. Disregarding the closet, he opens the door to the utility room. No light, only one window high up in the far corner. He steps into the room, letting his vision adjust and sees a cord hanging down from a light bulb. Thorne is behind several cartons piled inside the door. The light comes on and the man faces away from him so he takes advantage of the element of surprise. Creeping toward the man's back, he grabs him in a blood choke hold. With pressure on the carotid artery, the blood flow to the brain is cut off and the man goes unconscious in thirty seconds. But not soon enough to stop him from instinctively kicking out and knocking over several paint cans piled by a workbench. They clatter on the concrete floor. Both Jo and man number two hear the commotion.

The second man calls out in an angry voice and runs to see what is happening. Jo hears the footsteps go past her toward the utility room and acts decisively. Sliding the door open, she sees the man raising a truncheon to strike Thorne. She connects with the base of his neck with her pistol and knocks him to the floor. He won't be out long.

Both Jo and Thorne stand over the downed men. Thorne grins at his partner.

"Those coveralls and the van outside are looking like our way out of here right now. Let's tie them up and scram."

"Good idea."

They use twine found on the bench to tie their ankles and wrists and pull the men back-to-back into a sitting position. But not before Thorne removes one of the men's coveralls and his hat which is similar to Jo's but without the insignia. He dons the disguise and they run to the van. Thorne maneuvers it close to the guard house and parks in an empty slot. Standing in the back both he and Jo remove the coveralls, toss the hats and replace the visitor's badges on them. Going out the back door, they walk perpendicular from the van and once on a sidewalk, reach the guard house where they leave the badges and the base. There is a museum and a visitor's area on the base and it's not uncommon for tourists to visit. They are not questioned when they leave.

Li is nowhere around. Achara paces beside the Mitsubishi Pajero rented an hour ago. It's black and sleek, almost like it's happy to be there. But Achara is not. When she spies Jo and Adam walking from the guardhouse, she jumps in, starts it up and moves close enough for them to jump in. Adam directs Jo to the front seat and gets in the back. Achara nods her head toward the back seat.

"Did he give you a surprise Jo?"

"Oh yeah. The last person I expected to show up but I'm glad he did."

Jo turns to look at Adam.

"I'm waiting for that explanation."

Achara pulls out of the parking lot and heads south. Jo notices that Achara's vehicle with the busted radiator is gone. She is about to ask but Achara talks first.

"Let's go back to my place. I want to check if the police are gone. I want to know what's going on first Jo. What did you discover? Who's the asshole in the Air Force behind this?"

Jo starts by telling her of Bunnag, finding the dead body, the uniformed man leaving and what he looks like. She went on to describe Thorne's arrival and the subsequent subduing of the men coming to collect the body. When they get to the house, a white van is parked in front, on the wrong side of the street. The driver's door is open and a uniformed man is walking to the house. No cops around. Crime tape still across the front. Jo tells Achara to pull over out of sight.

"That's the man that killed Bunnag. What's he doing here?"

"Bunnag must've told him. We can wait it out and follow them. See if he'll lead us to his accomplices. I expect they'll be freaking out right now."

Jo nods in agreement.

"Let's do that and in the meantime, tell me what you're doing here Thorne."

"I came to take you home."

# CHAPTER 18

## NINETY MINUTES EARLIER.

Adam Thorne departs from the taxi in front of Jo's cottage. He's one of the two people that knows where she is. More than partners in the past, they're good friends. He came to Thailand to bring her back to Canada, or rather to try and talk her into returning to clear her name.

Walking up on the front porch, he sees the broken window in the door and waits, thinking there might be an intruder in the cottage. No movement or sound comes from within. Walking slowly to the side, he peeks in. Not seeing anyone, he opens the door.

"Anybody home?"

No answer. He looks around. Realizing no one is here and the contents of the bedroom in disarray, he thinks Jo may have left in a hurry. Worried now, he looks for clues to her whereabouts. The only thing he finds is a piece of note paper on the floor beside the phone. On it is written in bold letters, **Achara Jones PI** and a phone number. He dials the number and is directed to an answering service. Explaining who he is, he hangs up and decides he'll find the office and go there. The phone rings. The voice sounds desperate. He listens for several minutes and responds.

"I don't know where it is but I have a taxi waiting. I'll meet you there shortly."

Eight minutes later, he meets Achara Jones and Lance Corporal Li at the parking lot by the base. After an explanation, he shows them his passport and police ID. He gets funny looks from the two of them when he starts laughing.

"I don't mean to sound like I'm taking this lightly, but knowing Jo, she's either on top of things or tied up somewhere waiting for her Prince

Charming, which just happens to be me. It won't be the first time I've gotten her out of trouble. Best part is they won't be expecting me. Now, can either of you two get me on base? And I need a gun."

# CHAPTER 19

Jo looks at her friend with a raised brow.

"Take me home?"

"Well, sort of. I had a chat with…"

Their conversation is interrupted by Achara. They're about seventy meters from her house when a black Chevrolet Captiva, looking extremely official, pulls into her driveway. The man gets out and joins Wattana at the door.

"Oh, oh… looks like we have company. You two stay here, I'm going to sneak around the back and check it out."

Achara has the door open when Jo grabs her shoulder. The men are returning to the Chevy.

"Wait Achara. Who's the man with Bunnag's killer?"

Achara sits back.

"It's Police Chief Ounsamai. They call him Mao because he looks like a mouse. This is not good. They've come looking for the children I bet."

Thorne is sizing things up with the limited information he's garnered. The three of them are watching the two men sitting in the parked vehicle. Angry faces and gesturing hands, they look like they're arguing.

"Or for you and Jo. You two are the only loose ends, aren't you?"

Achara looks back at Thorne with a look on her face that she's come to a similar conclusion.

"No, we're not. I told Lance Corporal Li about this. He's already been warned off the case. We don't know how deep this goes, who else is involved."

Jo thinks of the small children, the life they may have been forced to live.

"How much higher can it go? You said this is the police chief? He can send his investigators in all kinds of directions or quash it all. Li is only a Lance Corporal. What could he do? I think it's up to us Achara."

"I know Jo, but we need proof."

Thorne points to the Chevy.

"Look, they're leaving. Let's follow them and be careful. Stay back and keep them in sight."

Achara waits for another car to go by her, keeping the car in sight. It moves out of the residential area and takes the main highway following the bay. The police station and the Air Base are in the opposite direction. The two men are heading north, away from Kiri Khan. Thicker traffic makes it easier to follow them unnoticed. Jo watches the properties get bigger; the houses statelier with tall palms, manicured lawns and winding driveways.

"Where could they be going Achara? This area looks a little beyond the means of an officer or a police chief."

"Maybe that's why they buy and sell children."

# CHAPTER 20

Group Captain Wattana pushes the sun visor down to shade his eyes from the setting sun. Glancing at his watch, he sees it's almost three o'clock. He has to be back on base by six. They need to take care of this problem right now. He hates having to go to Mongkut. The man is ruthless. But he and Ounsamai have nowhere else to turn. Slamming his fist on the steering wheel, he shouts at his passenger.

"We have to get rid of Li. The two women too. And you must cover this up."

Ounsamai is trying to control his anger, his oval face red and slick with worry.

"You think it's that easy. We already have enough dead bodies to account for. Another one washed up on shore this afternoon. One of Bunnag's henchmen. And what are you doing about Bunnag's body?"

Wattana waves him off.

"Don't worry about that. Two of my inner-circle are looking after it. He'll be dogmeat by now."

"I hate going to Mongkut with this. He's going to be pissed. You know what his temper's like, why they call him Singto?"

Ounsamai reflects on that. Lion is a fitting name for a beast that kills indiscriminately. Although he knows he's a small man on the totem pole, he has kept Mongkut's people out of the fire enough times to warrant his importance. He's not scared of Prawat Mongkut.

"I'll deal with him. I know where a few skeletons are hidden."

# CHAPTER 21

A high-end shopping area breaks the monotony of wealthy homes. The perfume of tender blossoms hangs thickly in the air from dozens of graceful trees shading luscious gardens and hand laid brick walkways, an overall atmosphere of money. Off to the far side on a separate property, a long, low building fronted by a restaurant nestles amongst palms and strong branches splayed out like an umbrella, tall hedges separating it from the shops. The front has glass windows for ten meters before the building cuts to the left at an angle facing another parking lot. Here there is a cabaret style bar. Bronze and bright red bricks form the walls. Sculptures of Thai maidens and flowers in abundance grace the perimeter. Barely seen from the road, it offers patrons a certain degree of privacy.

The drinking establishment is not open to the public. Mainly empty at present, it only opens at ten in the evenings. It is membership only usually by invitation. The waiting list is composed of lawyers, politicians, doctors, entrepreneurs, a couple of judges and the wealthy. Thailand's top entertainers appear regularly. Only thirty new memberships are offered per year. They're coveted like gold bullion. The sign over the restaurant reads ของดานเต้ของ – *Dante's Inferno*. The bar has no sign but those in the know refer it to as the *Divine Comedy*. Mongkut owns it. He considers himself an intellectual and a reader of great works as well as devotee to Dante's words. Naturally his taste in art turns to Hieronymus Bosch and his detailed paintings, and other artists of the fifteenth century. He is also a predator.

More secretive and selective than the bar, is the operation in the back. Catering only to those with an endless stream of money and a perverted idea of sexual gratification. The rooms are all themed, some with chains and whips for those devoted to pain. Others are soft, sensuous, brightly colored, given only to lavish pleasure. The only commonality they have is the presence of children. Of the six rooms available, only two remain vacant. It's the middle of the afternoon.

Mongkut is showering in his own private suite. The young girl he recently deflowered has been returned to her watcher. His long hair is in lather and the muscles ripple on his forearm as he massages his head. Shorter than average, he has the torso of weightlifter and the ego of a fanatic. While standing under the showerhead, the jets rinsing his hair, a buzzer sounds on the intercom. Voice activated, Mongkut answers.

"This better be good. I said I didn't want to be disturbed."

A voice filled with impatience returns.

"I told them but Wattana insists he needs to see you right away. Ounsamai is with him."

Mongkut shakes his head. It's not a good sign they're here together. Something must have gone wrong with the shipment. That's the last thing he needs right now.

"Take them into my office. Give them something to drink. I'll be there shortly."

He towels off, admiring himself in the floor to ceiling mirror in the bedroom. Grabbing a pair of walking shorts and a black T-shirt, he slips on a pair of sandals and tucks a gun in his waistband just in case. He only trusts them so far. They are both hogs for the money. More so for the times he lets them taste the wares. They're among the sickest of his dogs. He almost wishes he didn't need them.

The front office is more like a living room. One outer room leads to the back of the main area and makes up one of two admittance points to the private premises. The other is a guarded entry at the rear, opening to a private parking lot. Ounsamai and Wattana are standing at a bar lining one corner on the back wall with open bottles of local beer untouched in front of them. The chief is wringing his hands and loosening his shirt collar. After the guard leaves them, Mongkut enters through a side door. He confronts the two men and their silence tells him it's not good news. Lifting a finger for them to wait, he pours himself an ounce of 100-year-old cognac from a Baccarat crystal decanter.

"Ok, tell me."

# CHAPTER 22

Achara, Jo and Thorne pull into the shopping area in time to see the Chevrolet pull into the nearly vacant parking lot by the bar side. The two men get out and after speaking briefly to a man at the door, enter the premises. The restaurant side is busy. They leave their vehicle in the main parking lot at the rear of the mall. Thorne offers to check the rear of the building while the two women case the front. The right side of the building has a narrow lawn dotted with shrubs and flowerbeds between the wall and the hedge that separates it from the commercial grounds. The tall palms are numerous and shadow the grounds. A thin man in a dark suit patrols the area. They agree to meet back by their vehicle in fifteen minutes.

Thorne is the first back and the ladies not far behind. He takes the lead.

"There's one man by a door in the back. There is a small parking lot with a gate, kinda private. Five vehicles with extremely high price tags. I took photos of the tags with my phone just in case. Another man by the side making rounds. They are both wearing jackets. If the place requires this kind of security, I assume they're armed. I didn't see any cameras."

Jo is off to Achara's right, confirming what they saw.

"Two men in the front. One near the door, which looks locked because Wattana and Ounsamai had to be buzzed in. The other shuffles about the edge of the building and the parking lot, no hurry or pattern. Looked like he had a cloth of some kind in his hand. We need to get in there."

Achara is shaking her head, gesturing with her hands.

"Not going to be easy, the bar is closed until ten tonight. If we want to get in, we'll have to force our way."

Both Jo and Thorne curl their hands into fists and smile. They're ok with that. Achara grins back.

"All right. Let me make a phone call first and then this is what we'll do."

Twelve minutes later the man patrolling the side and the man in the back are unconscious, bound and gagged at the edge of the forested property, hidden amongst the foliage. Thorne moves to the side of the restaurant to watch for anyone approaching the bar area. Jo has snuck around the back, now unwatched and crosses to the other side of the building, the bar side. Creeping through the foliage, shrubs and statuettes that line the left wall, she gets to the front. Unlike the restaurant, this section is all brick. To take the plainness away, a large mural consisting of champagne flutes, escaping bubbles, musical notes and laughing beautiful people, adorns the wall. Two wide, wood and opaque glass doors are three steps up from the walkway.

She sees the man at the front entrance resting his butt on the wrought iron railing, arms crossed, a bored look on his face. He's facing her but looking out to the parking lot, watching Achara approach his associate who is polishing a mint 1960 Edsel. Even at this distance, he can see that she looks fine. Jo draws her gun and waits four meters from the bottom step, hidden behind a hedge of brush hollies. She can also see Achara from this vantage point.

Achara strolls toward the man shining the car, adding a little sway to her walk. She's got on a trust-me smile. Jo watches her gesturing at him with her hands, pointing to the building. He's wiping his hands on the polishing cloth, grinning at her, shaking his head. He's a good six inches taller than her. His sport coat with its narrow waist likely wouldn't be able to button over broad chest. Jo can't hear the conversation but Achara must have said something funny because the man has his head back laughing in response.

Achara hits him in the throat. His hands go to his neck, eyes bulging. She grabs him by the ears and rams his head into her knee. He goes to the ground. At that the guard at the door becomes alert. He draws a long-barreled gun from inside his suit and shouts for her to stand down. Achara raises her hands and steps away from the car. She's hoping Jo or Thorne are on him. With pistol extended, he descends the steps to confront Achara. When he reaches the bottom, Jo squeezes through the slim branches and shoves her gun into his ribs. Not sure if he can understand English, he seems to understand *dead* and freezes. Achara hastens to cover him too, to stand directly in front of them. The man is Thai so Achara takes command.

"Lower the gun and give it to me."

His glares at her, his Adam's apple bobbing like a cork on a fishing line. He does as he's told.

"Now, be nice, be quiet. The lady beside you doesn't like bad people. She has a mean temper. Acts first and asks questions later, know what I mean?"

A quick nod. At this point, Thorne sees what's happening and rushes over keeping his back to them while still watching the parking lot. Achara points to the keys clipped to the man's belt.

"Give those to me. Which one opens the door?"

He's stuttering when he replies. More scared of Mongkut then these three.

"I… i…it's an electronic lock, c… controlled inside. These… these only work inside."

"How many are in there?"

"Only boss and some guests."

Jo digs the gun deep enough that the edge of the sight cuts through his shirt and scratches a rib.

"Ok… ok… two more, one inside door, one in back at office."

"You're going to get us in there. You make it so I go in first, then you with my friend here steering you and holding your miserable life in her hands. Thorne, you watch our backs."

The man pushes a button on the wall-mounted intercom. And tells the screen he needs to use the washroom. The buzzer sounds and Achara enters with the other two right behind her. The man inside is Caucasian with the blondish hair and blue eyes of a Scandinavian. He meets them at the door with hands open, palms up. Eyeing the unfamiliar women, he gives his partner a questioning look. Before either of them can reply, Achara whips out the first man's gun which has s silencer and sticks it in blue eye's face, telling him to not move. Reacting with no hesitation, he ducks and reaches for his own weapon, slick on the draw. Not fast enough. The spit from Achara's borrowed gun echoes in the empty space and gets lost in the acoustic tiles lining the ceiling. The bullet ruptures his heart.

Jo's captive is stunned by the action and jumps back toward Jo. She takes advantage of the man's distraction and whacks him on the side of his head with her gun. He falls directly on top of his dead friend.

"Shit Achara, this is getting intense."

"Yeah, well it was him or me. Stupid man. He should've stayed still. I'm doing him a favor. A white boy like that would've been somebody's pin cushion in prison."

They use the two men's neckties to bind Guard One and stuff his pocket hanky in his mouth. Thorn is posted to watch the front door. The women make their way through the table and chairs to the door in the back. The design is very modern, very Swedish. Chrome and a black and white theme dominate the premises. The only color is the reproductions of famous paintings inspired by Dante's poetry, most of the *Inferno*. The serving area is long, gleaming with dark lacquer and glistening metal. Two sunken bulbs of low wattage over the bar light the premises, leaving the walls in shadow.

Off to the right is an alcove. On the exterior wall there is a fire door with a red exit sign above emitting a dull reddish glow. A push bar has a yellow decal above it warning that pushing it will cause an alarm to go off. On the left there are three doors. With their backs to the viewer and only twenty centimeters tall, a naked woman is posted on one, a naked man on another. A third door is identified with only the word Private. It's much fancier than the other two. Jo points to it and Achara comes to her side. In a whisper Jo wonders what's on the other side.

"Shall we try this one?"

Achara holds out her weapon. So does Jo as she reaches for the knob. It's locked. Getting a nod from Achara, Jo raps lightly on the door twice. They only wait ten seconds before a slight woman opens the door. Jo bursts in, driving it open further and sending the woman to the floor. Achara is about to step in behind Jo, when the woman on her downward fall kicks out at Jo's knees, knocking her off balance. Sitting up, the woman draws a short-stubbed gun from an ankle holster. Aiming at Jo, she's about to pull the trigger when Achara steps in and kicks the woman in the ribs. The gun goes off, the noise almost deafening in the small room. The shot is wild. Jo recovers and with her gun clutched tightly, she shoots the woman in the stomach. Everyone in the building hears the shots.

# CHAPTER 23

Mongkut drops his glass on the hardwood floor. Wattana crouches behind a lounge chair. Ounsamai jumps from his bar stool and pulls out his side arm. Kneeling on the floor, he points towards the noise with both hands on his gun. Mongkut reaches behind the bar and removes a handgun. They can hear the moans of the injured woman, and voices.

Jo and Achara stand on each side of the only other door. Achara yells out a bluff.

"Give yourselves up. We have the place surrounded and all your men are dead."

Mongkut is not one to give up. He fires several shots through the wall where he thinks the voice is. The bullets skim by Achara's head. One grazes the muscle on her thigh. Gasping with pain she falls, her weapon clattering on the tiled floor. She falls next to the woman who has bleed out and lies lifeless. Jo turns toward the wall and fires back. Two shots shatter the mirror over the bar. The other goes through the lounge chair and hits Wattana in the lung, throwing him down on his back. Jo stands back and kicks at the door. Achara retrieves her gun and kneels painfully at the opening, shooting blindly to cover Jo, who fires at Mongkut. His weapon flies free and he clutches his damaged hand, screaming curses. A second shot takes him in knee. Ounsamai is lying prone and aims at Jo as one of Achara's bullets buries itself in his shoulder.

Several rooms hold under-aged children who have been sexually abused by older men, anytime of the day, twenty-four hours a day. Interrupted by the sounds, men in rooms one, two, three and four hastily pull their clothes on making for the back door. An alarm starts blaring and the rise of police sirens in the background grows menacingly.

Thorne hear the shots and rushes through the cabaret, only to find Jo disappearing into another door in the back. He stops to help Achara. Ripping a phone cord from the desk, he applies a tourniquet to her leg. They ignore the cries of the other men. He and Achara can hear Jo yelling.

"No… no. How terrible!"

78

# CHAPTER 24

An hour later, Lance Corporal Li, Achara, Jo and Adam Thorne are standing next to Li's patrol car, the door open, revolving lights coloring the shadows. Four ambulances are parked in front. Mongkut is in one, Ounsamai in another, with the two others for the children, one a ten-year-old girl with whip marks on her back, the other an eleven-year-old boy with welts on his backside. Attendants are closing the doors and preparing to leave.

The other men are handcuffed and waiting in the back seat of the cruisers. Hearses are coming for the dead, one of which is Wattana, the other the woman. A crowd is gathered to the side, controlled by two beat cops. Three other police vehicles are parked helter-skelter in front. One is a van with several members of a swat team packing up. The deputy chief and several minions are directing things by the main door.

Jo's face is tear stained; her eyes still glassy. She steps toward Li.

"What about the children? How many were there?"

"There were seven altogether. They're being tended to right now by two female police officers in the back. We're waiting for people from the Child Protection Committee to arrive and take them to a safe place."

Achara has been bandaged by the EMTs and limps beside Jo. Thorne stands behind them listening to the conversation before he speaks up.

"What's going to happen to these people?"

"They'll be charged, of course. Kept under guard if they need hospitalization, which I think will definitely be the case with Ounsamai. I expect Mongkut's lawyers will try to arrange bail but there's enough evidence here to make that difficult. We ran the tags you photographed. This is going to make a huge stink. One is a well-known property developer and the other is the Provincial Governor. Not good. Excuse me ladies."

He walks close to Thorne, his back to the commotion.

"Give me the gun I lent you Thorne. Do it slowly. No reason for you to be involved more than you are."

Thorne does so and stands back. Li slips gun and holster in a side trouser pocket. Jo is still stricken by her discovery of the children in the bedrooms.

"What now Li? Is this where it ends?"

"I don't know Jo. I don't think we'll ever stop the flow of children from our country or the abuse and slavery we see here."

He points to the deputy chief that is studying them from the distance.

"Kanchana is a good man. He'll clean this up. He's had his suspicions before and he'll look good with all this. Good enough to let you people walk. Leave this behind you. Now go, get out of here while you can."

The three of them start for their own vehicle at the mall when Li taps Jo on the shoulder.

"A minute Ms. Delaney. Or should I say Naylor?"

Jo stares at him defiantly, remaining silent.

"I could bring you in you know? There's an extradition treaty with Canada and we believe that whatever is punishable in Canada is likely the same here."

They wait a few moments in silence. Jo, uncertain what to say remains quiet, knowing that's often the best policy. Li thinking of the consequences of what he's about to do.

"I know you already gave the gun you were using to Achara and she accepted all responsibility. I also know that this might not have been discovered except for your involvement. I'm not worried about Achara, she knows the lay of the land but you... well, I think it best that you leave Thailand at the first opportunity. There's going to be people that will lose a lot of face as well as a lot of money because this operation is shut down. They'll be hunting for those responsible. Go home with your partner. Do it as soon as you can."

Jo knows he right. She reaches out to shake his hand.

"Thank you, Lance Corporal LI."

# CHAPTER 25

It's almost nine PM by the time they all arrive back at Jo's cottage where they decided to spend the night. Achara's place is in no shape for habitation at present. The windows that were shattered have been boarded up by a handy neighbour. Blood still decorates the wall and the floor. Not a good place for kids.

Achara is carrying Malai, who is dead asleep, into the cottage. Worn out from the outdoor activities her care keepers put them through today, she was asleep when they picked up her and Dek Lek. Clad in flannel pajamas, she has the sweetest demeanor. Innocence radiant in the untroubled face. Jo drops her bag on the floor then points to the couch.

"Put her there Achara. The coffee beans and grinder are in the second cabinet over the sink Adam. I know you like your coffee and I could use a jolt of caffeine right now. Dek Lek, take your pack honey and get ready for bed. I know you're tired."

"What you do?"

Jo smiles down at her small friend. She's going to do the part she likes best.

"I'm taking Malai to her mother. I called her on our way over and they're waiting for her."

"Can I come? I help find her."

Jo pulls her close to her side, arm around her shoulder. Dek Lek staring up at her with mischief in her eyes.

"Of course, you can. You helped a lot."

"I need to shower and change. I've been in these dingy and dusty clothes all day. Dek lek, why don't you help Achara get Malai dressed. Put on that dress the Baumgardners bought her. And the sandals. Pack up her pajamas too, okay?"

When Jo comes out of the bedroom. Thorne and Achara are sharing a

81

mug of coffee, chatting away. Dek Lek is sitting on the floor beside the coffee table with Malai on her knees playing tic tac toe on Jo's note pad. They all stop and look up at her. Wearing her beige knee length shorts, a red sleeveless tee shirt, floppy leather sandals, she's looking more like a tourist than a man chaser. Thorne does a wolf whistle.

"That tan looks good on you Jo."

"Thank you, kind sir. Now if you too can tolerate each other for an hour or so, we'll be on our way."

Achara and Thorne wave a toast with their mugs.

"Have fun!"

Fifteen minutes later, Jo turns into the driveway. It's the sign everyone needs. The porch light comes on and Preeda bursts from inside, rushing toward the car. Arms open, a grin of relief and tears caress her cheeks. Malia spies her mother and with a scream of delight, fumbles to get out. The two meet in the middle of the short lawn. Preeda on her knees, clasping her daughter tightly, Malai aping her mother and crying too. Both crooning endearments. The uncle and aunt and cousins pour out, surrounding Malai and Preeda with shouts of elation.

Jo and Dek Lek stand outside the car watching the happy reunion. Both bearing impossible grins. Jo concentrates on Preeda and tries to imagine the joy she's feeling with the safe return of her child. She remembers once before when she and Thorne found a lost girl in an industrial park a few years ago. She was there when the little girl and her parents were united. The same emotions filled the air, the same tears of happiness, the same rush of relief as these people now. She misses being a cop. She's thinking maybe going back with Adam might be the right thing to do. But her meandering thoughts are interrupted when arms circle her.

Preeda has her head on Jo's chest, her arms holding her benefactor in the tightest of hugs. Over and over in her mother tongue she thanks Jo. Jo too has a tear at the edge of her eyelid. Preeda backs off. Jo will never forget the shine in her eyes. They don't need language to communicate. Jo feels the gratitude which is better than words. Preeda turns back to her daughter and Jo waves to Dek Lek to get back in the car. Before she can, Malai breaks from the crowd and scoots over the Dek Lek to hug her closely. Surprised by the affection, Dek Lek hugs her back and starts laughing. Malai starts laughing in return followed by Preeda and soon everyone is chuckling, some not knowing why. The joy is infectious.

Waving goodbye to everybody, Jo and Dek Lek turn to walk back to the car. Dek Lek reaches over and takes Jo's hand, squeezing it tight. Jo looks down at the pretty girl. There are so many changes in such a short time. She squeezes back and looks away. She doesn't want Dek Lek to see the glaze in her eyes. Jo hates what she has to do.

# CHAPTER 26

All four of them are packed into Achara's rental - Jo, Dek Lek, Thorne and Achara, who is driving. It's a few minutes after nine in the morning. Thursday, January 9th. The sun is behind a grey wall of cloud huddled on the horizon and crowned with a pink tiara. A clear blue sky follows them east. The weather forecaster called for a bright but hotter than average day. Gray day, rainy day or sunshine, it doesn't matter to them. They're all in a downcast mood, except for Thorne. He's confident Jo will follow him back to Canada. They're heading for U-Tapao International Airport. Thorne has an open ticket and he is catching a flight to Bangkok at 12:45 pm.

Jo called early in the morning from the beach when everyone else was sleeping to make her reservation. In a secret compartment in her bag, she still has her Jo Naylor passport, ID and banking and credit cards. Jo Delany's assets have all been cancelled and like the alias dumped. Today, she's travelling as herself. After two hours on the road, they pull into the airport. It's a long low building made of greyish white stucco. The ever-present palm trees line the sidewalk and offer some shade from the sun that has finally broken from it's cloud cover. The clamor of a plane landing, travellers, horns honking and vendors shouting greet Thorne and Jo when they get out of Achara's car. She's pulled over in a ten-minute dropping off area.

Dek Lek is the last to get out. Sullen and moody, she's been quiet all morning since Jo told her she was leaving. However, seemingly over her crying spell, she runs to hug Jo. Her head comes up to Jo's chest and her arms reach around Jo's waist. Jo does all she can to hold back the tears as she wants to be strong for Dek Lek. Achara approaches them and puts her hand on Dek Lek's shoulder.

"C'mon dear, they have a plane to catch."

Jo kneels and holds Dek Lek by the forearms. The little girl's lost look almost breaks her heart. She looks over at Achara for reassurance. A nod and closed mouth smile say it's good. Jo looks her tiny friend in the eyes.

"You know I have to leave. Bad people might come looking for me. We wouldn't be safe. Tell me you understand."

"I wish I could go too."

"I know but that's impossible. Achara will take care of you Dek Lek. She'll find you a good mother and father. Promise me you'll be good."

She nods and rubs an errant tear from her cheek and stands back beside Achara. Jo is speechless. Rising she looks to Achara. Scared to talk, she mouths a silent thank you. Achara reaches over to hug Jo.

"Good luck Jo. I'm glad I met you. Although I'm not sure I want to work for you again. You're too much trouble."

The sarcasm works and everyone chuckles. She hugs Adam and wishes him well. Thorne gives Dek Lek his pocket knife. It's small and slick and over seventy years old.

"This was my dad's. I think you're big enough to have your own."

Dek Lek hugs him and turns back to the car. Before they head into the airport, Achara eyes them both.

"Anytime you're in Thailand, my door's always open. I'm always here if you need me. Understand?"

They both nod and wave goodbye.

Jo and Adam go to separate check-in desks. She has one bag and her backpack. Adam has a carry-on and goes through quickly. Adam's flight is running a little late and scheduled boarding will be at 1PM. Jo on the other hand is told her flight is boarding at the very moment. She'd better hurry. Thorne is waiting for her at the coffee counter and as she approaches him, he lifts his chin toward the percolators and raises his brows. She waves no.

"I have to run Adam. My flight is boarding now."

He drops his cup of coffee on the floor. Eyes bulge, and his jaw drops at the surprise. He opens his hands.

"Boarding? Boarding now? Our flight is not until just before one."

She's shaking her head.

"I'm not going back to Canada with you Adam. I've changed my mind. There's nothing there for me but bad memories. I'm moving on.

"Aw Jo. Are you sure you want to do this?"

"Yeah. I know you mean well Adam, clearing my name and all. They want me, they can try finding me and haul me back. Maybe that'll be the next time I see you - when they send you to arrest me."

The attendant bends between them, cleaning up the dropped coffee and Adam steps back, putting his hands in his pockets. He's seen this look on Jo's face before. He knows he'll never convince her otherwise. Giving up, he steps around the young barista and envelopes Jo in a fierce hug. Like Preeda, no words are needed. He releases her, brushes the hair off his forehead.

"So, where you going?"

"Never mind. The less you know when you get back, the better. After I'm settled, I'll send you an email."

She looks at the overhead clock.

"I have to run. Goodbye Adam."

She hesitates.

"What will you say when you get back?"

He shrugs.

"I couldn't find her. Goodbye Jo."

She throws him a kiss and dashes off for her flight. Running past a magazine kiosk, a large glossy copy of a travel mag has a striking sunset with a steel tower on the cover. She grabs it, chucks too much money on the counter and trots to the departure gate. When she's seated in first class, her purse at her feet, her backpack in the overhead, she takes out her magazine and stares at the cover. A wide grin crosses her face. She runs her hand up and down the glossy surface as if she can feel the girders in the structure.

Almost in a whisper she reminds herself:

"I've always wanted to see the Eiffel Tower."

## ABOUT THE AUTHOR

Allan lives in Cocagne, New Brunswick, on the east coast of Canada, with his wife Gloria. A former woodworker and sales consultant, he now enjoys retirement.

Two of Allan Hudson's short stories received Honourable Mention in the Writer's Federation of New Brunswick
The Ship Breakers
In the Abyss

This is the second Jo Naylor adventure.

The third Darke Alexander adventure is completed. Publication is targeted for late 2021.
Work has begun on The Alexanders 1921 – 1930 Vol.2

He publishes a blog called South Branch Scribbler, where he posts short stories, interviews with authors, artists, and musicians. You can also find updates on his writing, novels and events.

www.southbranchscribbler.ca

Allan Hudson Author | Facebook

twitter.com/hudson_allan

www.goodreads.com/allanhudson

Manufactured by Amazon.ca
Bolton, ON

29252249R00058